Jeroen Bl

The Yellow House

A novel about Vincent van Gogh

Translated by Asja Novak

Holland Park Press London

Published by Holland Park Press 2017

Copyright © Jeroen Blokhuis 2017
English translation © Asja Novak 2017

First published in Dutch as *Place Lamartine*
by Holland Park Press in 2015

A CIP catalogue record for this book is
available from The British Library.

ISBN 978-1-907320-56-9

Cover designed by Reactive Graphics

Printed and bound by
CPI Group (UK) Ltd, Croydon CR0 4YY

www.hollandparkpress.co.uk

The Yellow House paints a fictional picture of Vincent van Gogh's life between August 1888 and December 1889 when he lived in Arles in Southern France and where he created many of his masterpieces.

Jeroen Blokhuis tells the story from van Gogh's point of view, from inside his mind, providing a fresh and revealing look at how this intriguing painter worked.

The Vincent in this novel very much tries to fit in, but is often baffled by how people react. It is almost as if he can only express himself through his paintings, which in turn flummox the public.

At this point, Van Gogh has fled from the dark sombre Netherlands of his youth, from Paris, and even from his best friend and beloved brother Theo, in search of the light, the sun of the South. The yellow house in Place Lamartine becomes his refuge but what about his hope of setting up an atelier with other painters, of making friends, and having a sense of belonging?

AUGUST 1888

I've now read the article in *l'Intransigeant* twice and I slam the newspaper onto the table; I want to discuss it further but there's no one here to join in. Yes, two customers who never give me a second look and are now at a table drinking wine with the prostitutes. And that man who has also been eating on his own, but hates me. Joseph, then. He's walking around; I call him and point out the article but he is busy and keeps his distance.

Outside the sun is still bright; inside, in the narrow café, it is dark. The air here has a certain chill. At the back is the bar, full of the glasses Joseph's wife Marie polished this afternoon. She isn't here now. Next to the bar is the low door to the kitchen. In the middle, on the wooden floor, a pool table. I look at the newspaper. The photo of the *maison*. A few days ago, when I was walking along there late in the evening, a group of people were standing in the street. Ordinary citizens of Arles, who ought to have long since been asleep, and a few girls and the *patron*. And only now, after I've read about what has happened, do I see what was written on their faces: the sinking sensation of a murder. All that blood and despair in their midst, and now they had to stand out in the cold, waiting until the gendarmes had finally resolved everything.

The newspaper article is not so much about the murder as it is about what happened afterwards: the Italian suspects, and how all the Italian seasonal workers have been driven out of the city and how the residents showed their aggressive side, and how peace has since been restored. Have I noticed any of this? I haven't heard any rumours or seen any patrols; I haven't heard anyone talking about it. I was painting the entire time. This is the first meal I've had in three days. I missed it and now I want to conjure it up again but I can't manage to reconcile what little I saw

– those faces outside, the scantily dressed girls, the flickering lights, the door with the gendarme on guard – with the description in the paper. Joseph then comes up to me, thank God, and I want to ask him to explain everything to me in minute detail – if anyone knows, it's him. I'm already poking at the article with my finger but he doesn't react immediately. He's got something better in mind, I see it in the way he frowns. Joseph in his beige trousers and jacket, his summer suit. Why is he wearing that suit now? It looks even tighter on his sausage-like torso, and the worn patches are turning a shiny yellow. He's going to involve me in the situation, one way or another.

'You have to do something,' Joseph says. He's put his hand on my shoulder.

Do something? I don't want to take his bait too soon. 'It was delicious,' I say, 'the soup was delicious.' His breath smells like carrots, potatoes, wine, thyme; he has just eaten some of that soup himself.

'You have to do something, you have to go with those lads,' Joseph says, 'Benoît and Michel have to have someone else with them. There are still two more Italians, you have to go and get them. I would've gone myself, but does it look like I can leave now?' He gestures around, as if the café is full of children. Now I notice the two men standing by the door; they seem to be conferring and occasionally cast darting glances across to either side of the street.

Go and get them. They've chased all the Italians from the city. Except these two survivors.

'They want to go now,' Joseph says.

Of course I actually belong with them, the Italians, but I'm going to join the stronger side, strength in numbers. Without thinking, take the easy way out – so be it. I wouldn't need anything else, I could even give up my painting. I've already stood up.

I do know them, Benoît and Michel, although this is the first time I've seen them together. I come across Benoît in the evenings if there's drinking involved. Michel isn't

8

there at those times, he works in a butcher's shop and probably goes to bed early. They're not looking at me, they've sent Joseph as the messenger. Or maybe they haven't, and Joseph is getting them saddled with the Dutchman again. Joseph has well and truly enlisted them for this stint. They're still young. Benoît is standing with his arms crossed, with one foot already out the door. Michel's shoulders are bent and his head is pulled back, as if he's trying to keep a hood in place.

'Good,' I say. *'Bon. On y va.'*

Joseph nods, the men nod back. I go along. We're already on our way.

Because of the heat and the blinding light on the street, it feels as if I'm being carried along, but after a few good steps I feel strength return to my body. Benoît and Michel are walking in front of me and look back to check that I am still following. They're both short and have sticky black hair. Benoît has a lecherous face with fleshy cheeks and dark, impassioned eyes.

After the murder in the brothel, I can imagine men like Benoît and Michel and many others chasing all the Italians away from the city by throwing rocks. Migrant workers, in the factories and in the fields – they always have a bad name. They had never really been properly accepted; now they no longer beat around the bush in Arles. The men went on the prowl, the women encouraged them, that's how I imagine it. Of course there were leaders and people from the organisation. Joseph was part of it. Benoît and Michel are followers. Benoît had, by the way, been in the gendarmes, I suddenly remembered, that's what he told me one evening when I was really drunk. Now he's a working man himself and always walks in the street with a skip in his step, which naturally doesn't become a gendarme. He was there, in the brothel, when the Zouave was being stabbed by the Italians.

'What is the plan?' I ask. I have been working the whole day, I have other things to do, but they say: 'We've been

9

working all day too.' We walk through the park in the direction of the arena. The air is so different from that in the north. Against the background of the paleness infusing the evening, everything down here seems so heavy with colour, dripping, almost. And later on it's the opposite; from the faded city you look up into a deep night sky.

To walk through the city with a little band – I really like that. People seeing me with company. Fulfilling a function, however banal it may be. *Vincent often picks things up for Joseph. Vincent often helped. That thing with the Italians, Vincent was part of that too.* Later, Marie will see me coming back, or she will hear of it from Joseph, and then I shall become part of everyday memories.

Michel is completely different from Benoît. He is thin and stiff and cross-eyed. With every movement of his head, his eyes go a bit askew and then it takes them a moment to straighten back up. In the shop he uses this moment to brighten it up with a smile, but this time he is not smiling. Michel would be easy to paint, at least for me; despite his calm features, it would be a portrait of a restless man, restless from anxiety; he doesn't have it in him to live long.

I decide to speak to Benoît.

'What did it look like?' I ask him.

'What did what look like?'

'In there.'

He knew what I meant. He casts a cautious look at Michel, who has obviously already heard him tell the story once.

'I'll tell you what it looked like,' he says. 'It had such an impact on me. It's different from what you'd imagine.'

'I don't picture anything yet,' I say.

'You know what a Zouave looks like, with their pretty uniforms and their pretty caps. Now it was like he had been swimming, with his clothes and all, that's what it looked like. His clothes were soaking wet and glued to his body. That's what it looked like.'

A smile. Go on then.

'I was upstairs, of course; we were already getting a bit started in bed, but I still had my clothes on. Then I heard the shrieking and the screaming downstairs and I'm telling you honestly: I thought immediately of something horrible, I turned into some kind of wild animal, ready to defend myself. But by the time I'd run down the stairs everything was calm again, perfectly normal. And as I opened the door to the salon those two bastards walked past me. Of course I didn't know yet that it was those bastards, they walked away so calmly and casually. And then, in the salon, I saw the red, drenched Zouave. Blood, blood, blood, everywhere. The knife was still sticking out of his body, and another one was lying beside him. Everyone sat there, dead silent, no one moved. I look around. I pointed at a few people. I said: "You go and get a doctor, you get the gendarmes." I asked them: "Was it those two fellows that just walked out, the Italians?" Everyone just nodded. I said: "Why didn't anyone go after them?"'

Michel was walking just in front of us but now he lets us catch up. Benoît turns to the two of us.

'That knife, which just stood there with only its narrow tip in his stomach, it could've fallen out so easily. I thought: I have to hold it in place, the knife, I have to hold the handle upright. But I didn't do it and it didn't fall out either. There wasn't a lot of blood coming from the wound. All of the blood had poured from his throat and his chest. Then we did eventually go back to try to catch the bastards, me and another fellow, we ran up and down through the whole city, but nothing, of course. And I was also really done with it by then, now I just wanted to go to bed with Rachel, but by the time I got back no one was allowed inside any longer. I stood there shouting "Rachel! Come, come, come!" It turned out she was standing right next to me! That whole time she was already outside. And so cold, oh boy.'

That must have been about the time I walked past the place myself. I can't remember Benoît being there. Maybe

11

he was still in the middle of his chase then. 'No more fucking after that,' Benoît says. 'I tried again after a while but I couldn't think of anything apart from that knife. I really should have pulled that knife out, that's what I should've done, and not left it there in his stomach, quivering. I can't get it out of my head.'

I see the Zouaves occasionally walking inside and outside the city. They're mostly alone or in twos, never in a group as you would expect. Farmers. With their farmer's faces, they calmly stroll around undisturbed by the heat and not thinking back to what they have done in Indochina or Algeria; they'll soon find themselves in the thick of it again. At times when I see a fellow like that walking past, I follow him with my eyes, for as long as possible, to see the intense and almost ugly colours of his uniform and the warmth and the calmness of his face. They all have these calm, southern-looking faces. Now one of them is dead, murdered in the midst of that calmness, and that is appalling.

We arrive in the neighbourhood where the seasonal workers take shelter in pensions, alongside the local poor who consider themselves slightly superior to them. In the Rue l'Epin we suddenly slow down. We move towards one of the shabby-looking houses on the left-hand side, the one with the closed shutters, until we're almost directly in front of it. The first impression it gives is of being deserted, of a nest waiting for its next inhabitant, or for decay. But in similar houses in this street I see movement, forms or shapes, and Benoît gestures to us to walk around to the back of the house. Michel wants me walking behind him, but I feel an urge to be really doing something, so we walk hastily side by side. We're almost out of breath by the time we reach the small yard behind the house.

Behind the houses is a dusty strip of land where someone has tried to plant a garden. Dried-up garlic, withered stakes, ribbons that look like seaweed. We could crouch behind a wall, but then I think: it would be absurd to hide.

12

The Italians are the ones hiding. What will happen now? Is there a plan? There is no plan, or else they would have given me instructions.

'Are you sure they're here?' I whisper.

'They were seen here this morning,' says Michel.

Why aren't they long gone? There's nothing left for them in this city. They can only live in hiding here. Maybe they feel invincible. If we find these men later, I still don't know if I'll take part or if I'll decide to help the Italians. They are working men, they haven't murdered anyone. They work and they know nothing.

I'm on the other side now. Is that what I want? Michel walks abruptly over to the house, flings one of the shutters open and shouts. Inside there's a commotion and the crash of furniture falling over, and it seems that there's a body throwing itself against the shutters, but it's Benoît, who has stuck his head outside and says that we're arseholes, that we have to come inside and that there's nothing to be found there.

And yet the tension doesn't immediately dissipate. Inside, where it's dark and cold, Michel dashes straight upstairs; I stay and wait. The house is now abandoned but it has been inhabited by people who did not need very much. There is a table without chairs. A pitcher of water. Crumbs are scattered. There is a simple wooden staircase. I could live in this house. It's not big, but big enough. I do my painting outdoors anyway and in here I could seek warmth and quiet. If it's good enough for migrant workers, then it's also good enough for me. To sit on the floorboards. Write at the rough wooden table, in the spot that's already worn smooth. Why would people stay in a place like this? For the normality of things, their familiarity and the reliability they provide. If this was where I lived, I would miss companionship less.

People have started to gather in front of the house, even some children. They're shouting. I had better stay away from the window. Soon they'll be throwing stones, that's the kind of thing they do around here, the children, but the adults too. Maybe it's the same everywhere, and maybe I should say that if at any point people are about to throw stones at other people, I'm always among those other people. I don't mind.

Everything is dusty. How quiet their stay here must have been, sitting on the ground in this room after work.

The people in the street are shouting up to where Benoît and Michel must be leaning out of the window. 'They've already gone, you're too late!'

'We can see that,' Benoît shouts. 'Tell us where they've gone!'

'That won't help anyway! At that pace of yours!'

'What about all of you then?! You're still just standing here, you haven't moved an inch!'

'Course not! After all, we knew you would come. "Oh, Benoît's coming," we were saying to each other! "Now it's all going to be fine!" Benoît the hero!'

'Where have they gone? That way?'

It goes on like this for a while. Benoît and Michel have come downstairs and are now talking to the people somewhat more calmly; suddenly, they set off again. I've missed what they said about where the Italians have gone, but I have an inkling.

We walk fast. At first we were walking normally, in the hope of finding something, but now we're more focused and we realise that we could be too late. If we're really going to the PLM railway yard, now we have to take the necessary diversions. As the crow flies it's no more than a hundred metres away. I wish I could clamber over the houses, across the roofs, jumping over anything I come across, and land at the site, but we have to go through the streets, streets that lead us out of our way, that end by the Alyschamps. And then across the sand. The tall trees provide some shade here, but still there are women strolling around with little black parasols lined with white lace, and gentlemen in beige hats. We dart through them. With one

14

quick glance around I try to take in the surroundings. The feeling of estrangement that I still had this evening during dinner is now gone, and my senses are sharpened. There's a sign, 'Paris-Lyon-Marseilles', at the perimeter of the site. No Entry. Through bushes, oak trees and oleanders, we enter the site. I've always imagined it as an open-air factory, but actually it looks more like a prairie. It's a flat open area with occasional low buildings or workshops, with rails and piles of materials clumped together. In the mornings and afternoons all kinds of work are done here, but now it's all deserted, left to the mayflies and beetles and the low rays of the evening sun. The walk here is across waste and debris, iron, stones. To paint here. All my plans could be realised in a flash. Flash, the work that I imagine, in front of me. Flash, the painting of the debris almost smouldering in the heat, with the poplar trees in the background. Flash, a cypress tree, a lonely cypress tree beside a road. Flash, the chimneys...

Then I hear footsteps, at the same speed, somewhere behind us. A Zouave. He is tall, with a strong torso. Red lips. He has his red cap in his hand and I can't see his blue cummerbund, but he's wearing his elegantly stitched jacket and the wide-legged trousers. He must be heading for the same destination as us, the same goal. I am scared that we are interfering and know that we must be wary. He knows that I am looking at him; he is not reacting, and in the meantime he is still walking in the same rhythm as us. Then I notice that he's holding in laughter, like someone trying to get one over on some old acquaintances, and the next moment he slaps his hand on Benoît's shoulder.

'Gentlemen!' he says. Benoît and Michel laugh back, they know him, they joke around for a bit, but they don't feel at ease. Caught red-handed. The presence of a Zouave, who was, after all, a comrade of the murdered one – perhaps even a friend – suddenly means they have less authority in this operation, maybe even none at all. The Zouave extends a hand, looks at me and says: 'The painter.'

15

I nod.

He introduces himself as Milliet. He points at me as if he is about to ask me something but decides that it will have to wait until later. 'Come on,' he says, 'there's work to be done.'

I walk next to the Zouave for a while, behind the two boys, showing off, like we've sent two children out in front of us. The iron, the workshops, tufts of grass, dustbins and red stones; in the evening sun everything looks as if it's been pressed deeper into the thick air.

Have I, again, changed sides now? Have I chosen to root for the winning team again? But Milliet doesn't demand anything from me. He is relaxed, this is a walk in the park for him after all that he's seen in Indochina. Benoît and Michel are walking, hunched together and gesturing at each other, but Milliet is strolling on smilingly and asks about my paintings. I don't really know what he wants to know but I tell him about the places close by where I've been painting. The Crau, the plain of Montmajour.

When Benoît and Michel walk to the left around a bridge, he whistles at them: there, go to the other side. He leads us to the edge of the site, where the small brick buildings for storing iron are – if you squat down you just about fit in, they are like tiny shepherd huts. The hectic feeling of almost being late is now gone. I trust the Zouave, and Benoît and Michel do too, or maybe they're just being obedient.

Then all becomes clear. They have been found.

They are in one of the huts.

Benoît and Michel walk, like cats with high shoulders and the corners of their mouths pulled wide, in a circle around one of the huts. There's shouting. A stocky man, older than I had imagined, comes out of the hut, bending down, followed by another who looks just like him but younger, a son, with his hands on his head. Everyone is about to start shouting. The Italians then suddenly turn around, pull two bags out of the hut and one of them

16

gestures at Benoît and Michel, and the other is looking at Milliet. Still, they start to walk away calmly – apparently there's nothing to fear any more – in their shoes with the laces tied all around and their stiff, black trousers. Their black hair is long and they walk at the pace of donkeys. Gypsies, that's what they are, actually. If it were up to me I'd let them walk away like that; let's shake their hands; they do have a hard night of walking ahead of them. But I look to Milliet. He decides what happens next.

Minutes go by. At least, that's what it seems like. Minutes since they came out of the hut. The two street watchmen of Arles have shuffled their feet. Then Benoît takes two, three, four steps and clouts the smallest Italian round the back of the head. Then he places this same hand on his hip and advances, chest puffed up, towards the man, and then hits him once more with his hand from behind, smack. Michel kicks him in the back. The Italian groans. The three are actually fighting now.

I can see the bent back of the Italian, and his clothes that have nearly been yanked off his body in all the pushing and shoving and his attempts to escape. Filthy, that back. And his clothes, those rags are foul too. He gasps like an animal whilst fighting, but to me he doesn't look properly scared; he doesn't fear what is coming, he is just trying to stop the pain. Benoît and Michel now hit him in the stomach, but suddenly he gets free and runs ten steps away. This must be the end now, I think, and it is. The second Italian has fought for a bit, but has gone running at the first chance and is waiting fifty metres further down, watching the freed man stumble across the path to join him. They stand together for a moment. Far enough away to be safe.

The shadow of a poplar tree falls across the path before them, and behind them as well; they stand in between, in a trail of light. Orange pebbles on the path – or are they perhaps pieces of glass? – reflect speckles of light and so it seems as if they're standing in broad daylight. But the evening has already set in, the sky is dull, and the cold rolls in like gas along the trees. It isn't easy to make out the figures of the men from here. Maybe they're examining each other's injuries, and comforting each other.

Benoît is standing, eyes squinting, and smoking a cigarette. Michel has gone to sit on a rock. Milliet suddenly gestures at something. The second Italian is heading our way, and I immediately understand: he's coming to pick up the bundle he lost in the fight, which is lying on the ground in front of me. All the tension returns. The image of the men in the distance almost gave me a feeling of tenderness, but once he approaches, the Italian gives me a baleful glare. His eyes are close to each other, he hesitates for a moment, snatches the bundle from the ground and quickly springs back to his feet. I realise my posture is the same as my father's: half turned away, one foot forward, ready to leave, to give his support to someone who deserves it – this one is done with you, he's already rejected you and uttered his curses.

Michel has picked up a rock. When he's noticed that all eyes are upon him, he picks up another one from the ground and stands there with the two of them in his hands like loaves of bread. The Italian now scurries off to his friend, panting and exhausted.

It doesn't go any further.

'We shit in your milk! Always! Wherever you might be!' Benoît and Michel are still shouting; meanwhile they're already walking to the other side, away, to the café where they'll take all the credit.

I see the Italians walking along the Alyschamps. Then they dart through the trees and are already practically outside the city. The poplars draw one's gaze upwards, where they're wafting in an invisible breeze.

Even so, I could still catch up with those two and kick their feet out from under them, I'm still so full of rage. The Zouave sees it in me. He's gazing up at the dull sky now, as if he needs to think up a plan for me.

'Come,' he says. We walk back. 'What do you think about that?' Without looking at me, he touches my arm to soothe me, but it doesn't work like that. I tell him. I explain to him what I think of it, that escape is never possible, and that is quite a long story and he listens quite calmly. Once or twice he asks me a question, but without interrupting me. I also tell him what compassion means; I managed that in any case, even if I can't remember how exactly I did it now, but it must be clear. The rest of it, probably not, that couldn't have been comprehensible.

'I understand,' he says nonetheless, 'yes, yes, I do understand.'

But he cannot know how the smallest memory, such as the image of my father, makes me suddenly shrivel. In the garden behind the family home, amidst the balsam blossoms, when I would crouch there for hours because I didn't want to go inside and would pop the plump seed pods with my fingers. And the Italians trudging away, those castaway people, oh, how could I ever explain to Milliet what all of that means, oh! But Milliet doesn't notice anything, or pays it no heed, and asks me if he can come with me next time, the next time I go painting in the Crau.

'All right,' I say, 'all right.'

This chat with Milliet has actually made me calmer.

The roadsides are full of cicadas. At first I walk with my hands behind my back but Milliet lets his arms swing down by his sides and then so do I. The dust creaks under our feet. This is a good pace, like this. Between the houses the insects have disappeared; here are the pigeons, sitting on top of the roofs. In the narrow streets it's already dark. Here and there a gaslight is burning and its light floats like a cloud. It's silent too. Only when we walk right past it can I hear the voices of the people on the terrace. They see us.

We've taken along a flask of milk, some bread and a sausage. Milliet is already hungry, but I would actually prefer to save it. 'All right, all right,' Milliet says. And he looks just as pleased as when he came to pick me up this morning. The Montmajour hill lies ahead of us, in the middle of the plain we have crossed. The monastery ruins sit on the top.

It isn't a difficult climb, but our pace is slowed because of all the things that we're carrying – paint box, travelling easel and perspective frame. As soon as we pass into the shadow of a tree, I take off my hat and Milliet his cap, and once we're back in the sun we put them straight back on. Our feet sweep across the sand, the pebbles, the scraps of vegetation on the path, material for snake-trails. The rocks form basins, like large open hands, where that almost white grit settles; that's how plains come into being. A giant storm could come and blow everything away and uncover the uneven bottom.

When we're almost on top, I leave the path to take a shortcut, and in between the shrubs, the *garrigue*, lies a dead animal. Flies are gathering on it. It is a dog. The head is turned backwards, its snout has turned pale, its fur looks melted. Milliet isn't surprised. At first glance the dog doesn't look wounded. Where its insides are exposed, flies and maggots have eaten away its skin. It's heavy set and of a breed I don't recognise. A hunting dog.

'Has someone left it here?' I ask. But Milliet thinks that's improbable.

'It just lay down here; this is a good place to await the end.'

The dog is a world of its own: pale pink, with dark stains the colour of old excrement and the flies picking at the tissue. Parts of bones are sticking out; it's clear that soon that will be the only thing left. Samson's riddle. Still, the smell is so revolting that we quickly walk on. Later Milliet says: 'We could've drawn that beautifully, it was a perfect subject,' and I compliment him; I had the same idea. On

20

the top I quickly find a spot where we can stand. 'This is a beautiful spot, Vincent,' Milliet says. He can look so grumpy, but his face also relaxes quickly, he can't hold back his cheerfulness. You can see the whole plain from here, all the way to the city.

'We need a few good rocks,' I say, 'to secure the easel.' We find four blocks on the slope, and then it's time for the perspective frame. I notice Milliet is keenly watching.

'Aha,' he says, 'finally! Finally I get to learn the secrets of the perspective frame.'

I set up the device and tighten it. 'We can begin,' I say. But Milliet has walked a bit further away and is looking out. I go and stand next to him. You can hear the mistral much sharper here, due to the acoustics of the rocks, but down below the wind is more unexpected and threatening. The plain is crossed by roads and paths, but there is no one there to move along them. This morning we came across a cart pulled through one of the fields by a horse, not on one of those roads, and near it there were also no people to be seen. Directly beneath us stand holm oaks, sheltered and silent. Behind them the vine branches sprawl. In the distance everything is moving in the wind, the fields of grain and maize are being swept around wildly and the cypresses dance like dervishes. It's green. From dark green, the greyish green of the holm oaks, to the lavender and velvet of the olive trees whose crowns seem to hover over the ground.

No people. Nature has no formulas or codes for me to get wrong.

Yellow, straw-yellow, white houses covered with red clay tiles. It is as if the land sympathises with my longing and my expectation to make a beginning here, to find a source – perhaps on my own and perhaps with friends. Milliet sees it too. He points, and in the windy distance I now see the train which is crossing through the landscape with a soft whistle, on rails tucked away behind the trees, behind the hedges, behind the dry stone walls and even behind the grass.

'Don't make me wait any longer,' says Milliet, nodding towards the perspective frame. I explain everything to him. We look through the frame; I show him how you transfer the planes to the paper. 'Flat', he repeats the word constantly when he's working, because I've used it. Flat, flat. 'I've never seen someone with such a thing,' he says.

'But you also haven't seen very many painters yet,' I say.

We work. An hour. He's struggling, and I didn't think he would be this bad. Now and then, I help him by drawing a line or pointing something out, so that it starts to at least resemble a drawing. But it is pitifully bad, there's no saving it. In the meantime, I tell him about everything, about colours, the modernists, that you can paint the sky pink. He finds that really interesting, striking for someone with so little talent.

After a while he gives up on his attempts and sits down on a rock. Not in the shade; he takes the sun well and, just like me, seems to enjoy sweating. He's smoking his pipe. He says: 'I'd do better to just watch you, how you do it.'

And a bit later: 'Don't grumble so much.' We both laugh at that.

And a bit later still: 'You too are a real modern painter, with your pink sky.' And I smear even more pink onto the canvas, here, there and there. 'Yes, yes, yes,' Milliet laughs.

The pink is truly magnificent. I apply it and then flatten it with my painting knife. It's going well. That's how it's done. I'm standing here, Milliet's sitting behind me, he's a soldier, a good friend, I could work like this for days, and even nights, we light a fire, Milliet and I and Theo and Lautrec and Bernard and Gauguin and all the others. Yes, people, yes, Theo, yes, aunts and uncles and ministers, that's how it's going to be. 'Sing a soldiers' song, will you?' I say. And Milliet sings, with a strong, sonorous voice. It's a song that evokes camaraderie, but a bit later I also hear in it the loneliness of a soldier like Milliet. That seems like a different lifetime. I paint in the rhythm of the song. Milliet's voice is carried across the plain; I stir through it with my paintbrush. I paint as if I was a researcher making one discovery after another.

Suddenly there's a low shout behind us. On the slope between us and the dead dog stands a short man, gesturing with his large hands. Next to him stands his son, he has to be: the same rough skin, the same widespread legs anchoring him to the rock. I know the boy. He runs along with the group of children who sometimes follow me here on the Crau and shout at me or throw stones. He's sucked in his lower lip and looks from me to Milliet and from Milliet to his father.

'What is that? Singing? The dog?' I can barely understand what the man is saying. 'My dog? What's the matter?'

Milliet has stood up and is now walking towards him with an outstretched hand, but the man is pointing at me.

'What? My dog?'

Milliet says something back. Smiles. For a moment lays his hand on the farmer's arm. It's impossible to hear what they're saying from here, the wind. They look at me.

This farmer isn't happy that I walk around here over the Crau, I know that much. They let their children do the work, but I know he'd like to throw a stone at my head himself, and maybe he'll do it.

The farmer talks. Milliet now listens, looking intently in my direction. The farmer's vicious words are changing the look in his eyes: he, too, now sees a madman pacing up and down through the fields, tormenting children and kicking dogs to death. Those are the farmer's words. As I realise this, I feel my insides dissolve. My face turns to stone, the rest just disappears, I am now only a face looking at them, and it keeps hardening and hardening.

The times when people laugh at you, or when those children chase after you, or when your father pushes you away – you just don't believe it, until you do. All those times, I've felt my soul dissolve and my face turn into a mask that gets thicker, ever thicker and harder, a callous mask, emptier with each second that they look at me. Only after they've taken their eyes off you and leave, when you're alone, does your face soften again. Then, you have to stretch your mouth wide and blink your eyes and rub your cheeks with your hands. And then you have to forget, that's the only way.

The two men approach me, the lad behind his father.

'Do we have anything for this man to drink?' says Milliet.

I turn around immediately and rummage through our things to see if there's still some milk or water. Why? I cannot gauge the situation and so I do what I'm told, damn it. There's a little bit of milk left. 'It's warm though,' I say and push the bottle into Milliet's hand. He brings it to the farmer, who drinks from it and wipes his mouth. He nods at me. He gives the bottle to the boy.

Milliet smiles again, as if he is enjoying our being together. 'C'est le chien du monsieur,' he says.

'I don't have anything to do with it,' I say, 'if that's what he's thinking.'

'Of course not,' says Milliet. 'But now that you're so quick to deny it, we have a suspect…' He laughs again. 'The dog left the farm a few days ago, they suspected it was ill. I believe that it went off to die.' Milliet has nothing to hide, that's one of his essential qualities. The man and the boy seem to blend into the landscape and the distance. Now that they've had something to drink and are waiting around, they don't know what to do with themselves, and I can imagine them having crossed the plain and climbed up here in the hope of finding their dog and how they are beside themselves now that everything has irrevocably turned out to be as they had suspected. Still, I cannot trust them. Even if I can now look into their souls a bit, later they might start throwing stones again.

A bit later we walk down the hill. 'If they want to bury

it, this dog has to be taken back at some point,' Milliet said, 'so I'll do it.' He carries the dog in his arms. He does it easily, even though the animal is heavy and the stench must be overwhelming. Milliet walks as if he's carrying out a higher order that always guides him. But he acknowledges no higher laws, only his own. He is free, he is guided by simple choices, by choices that he has made. 'I only protect my boys,' that's what he says about the wars in which he fights. The hunt for the Italians, that's the same principle for him. Protect his boys, cherish the women, discover life.

By now, the dog has turned stiff. Milliet has slung one arm around the neck of the animal, making its front paws stick out either side of his shoulders, and holds the other arm around its lower body. The head of the beast is pointed upwards, the nose in the air – the stance of someone clenching their jaw through intense pain. The flies have left the dog, but the maggots and other creatures are obviously still swarming inside the carcass.

I walk beside him. After ten minutes, I notice that his pace has slowed down. Soon, I should take the dog from him, but I wait until he gives a signal. Then, he'll have to carry the painting stuff. The farmer and his son are walking behind us. At first it irritated me, but now I think they're doing it on purpose: this way, we form a procession. I walk along, I belong – so it seems.

I would have liked it if Milliet had come to help me pick up my things, which are still stored in the boarding house at Rue de Cavalerie. Castre, the keeper of the boarding house, actually stole them from me by locking them away when I moved. With Milliet it would have been a calm and dignified situation, but he has left with his companions and now Roulin is walking with me.

A grotesque fellow, really, this Roulin. Gleaming eyes, a nose so flat that you don't even see it from the side and a beard that is narrow at the top and wide at the bottom, with waves like dog fur. 'I'll handle it, let me have a chat with the gentlemen...' that's how he talks. He is a post-man, sorry, post chief at the station, and is always in the Café de la Gare, drinking. He laughed his head off because I had my beard shaved off this morning, and he sees that as a sign of subservience.

He can't imagine that I didn't want to let my beard grow like his. We walk together to Rue de la Cavalerie. I tell him about all the legal actions I had to take against Castre. He thinks this interesting because it means that this is a serious conflict, a significant conflict, both Castre and I should have actually left it all down to him much earlier. But better late than never, as he would say.

Rue de Cavalerie is a narrow street with multiple boarding houses, of which Castre's is the smallest. The street is cloaked in morning shadow but the air is clear. Maybe I'll get lucky now, here in Arles. Maybe I've stumbled upon the right track. If you go to a new place, the peo-ple are still unburdened, they don't know me yet, and they are still open-minded. And then if you make no blunders and if you by chance meet the right people, like Roulin, who can introduce you anew, who talk about you, then all interactions are easier, then you don't cause discomfort, then it'll be okay. Yes. Then they forgive you things. Then you can become a part of their lives. That's a matter of luck. Maybe now it will be okay here too. The beginning was awry, it seemed to go wrong as quickly as at home or in Paris, where nothing really fell into place. Or wherever else. But now I have Milliet, whose company ensures that the farmers begin thinking of me as normal. I have Joseph and Marie Ginoux from the café, who tolerate me and ask me for help. I have Roulin, who helps me in getting things done and who is a well-respected figure. I now have my own house, which I'm going to turn into a studio. It's going well. As for Castre, who has kept hold of my things – Roulin thinks that I'm right, and together we're about to put an end to the situation.

We go in through a swing door. Castre and his staff are sitting in the dark bar-room; they all stand up when they spot us. Crossed arms. Castre, with his shirtsleeves rolled up and his apron, looks like a butcher, like the leader of a gang of butchers.

'Bonjour.' Castre is silent.

Roulin immediately sits down at the table and gestures to Castre that he should also sit down, but he is only interested in me and I say: 'You know what I've come for.'

'I shit in the milk of your mother and I shit in the milk of your so-called right.'

I'm a bit scared of him, but shouting helps, that makes him listen. And it's easy, once you've got used to it. 'I shit in the food that you cook, in which you shit yourself before selling it!'

Roulin has stood up again. 'Gentlemen, we are civilised people... Let us sit down, dear man, pour me a beer, would you. Or a cognac. Pour me something so that we can discuss this amongst ourselves like men.' I've already lost my patience. I go outside. I walk to the veranda at the back of the building, where my easel, my canvases, a few boxes and a suitcase are stored. What is he thinking, this Castre, what, God damn it, is he thinking, keeping my things in here? This is where all the courtyards meet. Grey roofs and walls of yellow, mineral-like stone. My room was just above here. Shortly after I came to Arles and had started living here, I saw light shimmer before my eyes, but now I no longer value this small view. At once, I think of my own house, my yellow house on the square.

Inside Roulin must have had some success, since no one has come after me yet. Castre, naturally, knows Roulin. It makes no difference to me what they're saying about me at the moment, I'll give them five minutes and then, come what may, I'll take these things back to my house.

I arranged with Roulin that I would paint his portrait. And one of his wife. 'And later of my little child,' he said. 'A painting of the little one, that's beautiful.'

'And you get them for free, of course,' I said.

'For free? No, you pay me. I pose, you pay.'

That's the sort of anecdote they're telling each other now, Castre and Roulin, and then embellished by Roulin and poisoned by Castre. But not a minute later, they come out on the veranda. 'Mr Van Gogh,' Roulin looks at Castre, 'Mr Castre,' and he looks at me, 'we have come to an agreement.'

A ridiculous agreement, that's clear at once. I'm allowed to take my possessions, but in return, Roulin and I are to bring 'some things' up from Castre's basement. What kind of things?

'Oh, just some crockery. And a piano.'

All right, we'll do it. But, first, I shout for a bit longer.

'I shit in your basement! I shit in your food! And I shit in your wife's snout!'

'And I shit on your paintings and in your paint and on your brushes and in your gob!'

Roulin smiles contentedly and guides us back inside. At the back of the bar-room Castre opens a trapdoor. The post chief and I go down the stairs.

'Where is this crockery?'

The basement is big and rectangular, but the ceiling is not high. We have to bend our heads and look at the room from under our eyebrows. On one side hang ducts and pipes. On the other side I see the piano, but no crockery. In a cabinet?

28

'In a chest. A grey chest.'

There it is. A chest as big as a person. Roulin has started lugging it.

'This is not reasonable,' I say to him. 'You've negotiated badly if we now have to drag a 300-kilo chest upstairs. I don't owe this man anything. Nothing.'

'You don't understand.'

I bend down and try to get a good grip on my side of the chest. This discussion leads nowhere.

'Diplomacy,' says Roulin. 'After your stay here we needed a good bit of diplomacy. It has nothing to do with being reasonable. Up!'

I grab the chest. It's really heavy, obviously. It is so heavy, it seems as if it possesses a power of its own and it wants to thrust us round the basement. We barely hold our ground. We walk, step by step. We climb the stairs, really slowly, me first, Roulin at the back. It's the heaviest for him at this point. Castre stands at the top of the stairs to hold the trapdoor open for us and is suspiciously eyeing the chest. He points to the kitchen, 'There, there,' and starts walking to the corner, 'this is where it goes, here!', meanwhile letting go of the trapdoor, which thunders down with a bang, and then a screech from Roulin. I almost let the chest fall but I manage to more or less put it down and Roulin hops around, cursing and raging. The trapdoor has fallen on his foot and now he's roaring, eyes closed, in pain.

'God damn it,' Castre says. 'Control yourself, man.'

Roulin goes quiet. But he continues to writhe. His foot could be broken, it wouldn't surprise me. On the other hand, he has sturdy shoes.

Roulin gasps. 'Pour me a beer,' he manages. He sits down and holds on to his foot tight like a treasure chest. Castre hesitates for a moment, but then ends up getting a glass anyway and putting it on the table. Roulin knocks back the beer with his eyes closed.

'That leaves the piano,' Castre says.

'Right,' says Roulin, 'the piano... You bring up the piano and I'll hold the trapdoor open.'

Castre starts shaking his head. 'I know what your plan is, Roulin, it's not going to happen. Besides, I didn't do it on purpose.'

'That's beside the point,' says Roulin. 'I'm not letting you drop that trapdoor on my other foot as well.'

'God damn it,' I say, 'someone, I don't care who, is now going to help me with the piano, otherwise I'm getting my things and leaving.'

Roulin has closed his eyes again and puts the glass to his mouth to let the last drop of beer slide down his throat. Castre sighs. 'Listen...' He starts to argue, but Roulin seems not to hear.

'Pour me another beer,' he says.

With that I'm released from any obligations, rightly or wrongly. I walk to the veranda. I tie a few canvases to the easel, tie the easel onto my back, pick up one of the boxes and walk through the bar-room, past the gentlemen, to whom I wish a pleasant afternoon, through the door and onto the street.

This is going to be a lovely stroll.

There is the sunlight that didn't enter the bar-room, but that touches everything in the street. There are the dry cobblestones. There is the Crau. I know all of it. I have seen all of this and will show it to you. Painters from the north, if you come here. Bernard, or just Gauguin. Look, there is the Rhône. Icy blue, sometimes; mostly ultramarine. The big sun. At night the stars are up there, you can take the train all the way up. And if you go along here, you arrive at a square, the square with the flowerbeds, the gardens, where in the twilight men and women can't keep their hands off each other. There they are, the flirtatious men of the South. And the women, the Arlésiennes. 'The painters have arrived, they're working together in the Studio of the South!' I put a table out on the square, the wooden table, and put bread on it, and wine and onions, and we eat

30

standing up, we're too restless to sit down, there's so much we need to tell and show each other, canvases standing around us, and yet more people come out to join us, all the people of Arles. 'Where are you going?' 'To the studio!' 'Is the table outside again? Are the painters outside?' The canvases lean against the houses so that everyone can look at them and see the colours, see all that's new and get used to it. 'The table is out again, the painters are working'; everyone brings a bottle, take that soup, come, to Vincent's table.

Bernard might come. Lautrec. Others who I don't know yet. Maybe only Gauguin will come. Because he is coming, for sure. He's still holding off a bit, he's trying to get the best business deal, that's why he is holding out, that's why he keeps responding so late. If I think about him, I can picture him like this: on a cliff in Brittany, looking out over the grey water, new ideas growing in his head, knowing that only in the South can he let them break loose, and if not in Tahiti, then in the Midi. That Van Gogh is right, he'll think. I'll show Gauguin everything, and he'll take care of things. I'll furnish his room with everything I know here, as I see it; they're only paintings, mere distillations. But Gauguin will know what I mean. 'Come,' he will say, 'let's try it together.'

When I arrive at the square with my stuff on my back and the box in my arms, I look at my new little house and I cannot help feeling moved. The walls have been painted soft yellow again, and the shutters green. It is modest, but fresh and pleasant and youthful.

I bring the things into our yellow house. I open the shutters of our yellow house. I arrange the things in different rooms and then leave our house again, going into the square, towards Rue de la Cavalerie to pick up the rest. It's lovely to walk freely with empty hands.

In the boarding house there's nothing to be seen. And nothing to be heard; apparently they're not arguing any more. They're sitting in the bar-room. I thought as much.

Roulin's talking again. Red-faced, he looks straight at me, but not until I stand next to him and pat him on the shoulder, does he recognise me.

'Vincent!' he says. 'It's all OK!'

'Excellent,' I say.

October 1888

Everything is ready, but it is still so early. The dawn hasn't lifted yet. It's raining. It is the first cold day. And today he has arrived. He walks up the stairs in front of me. His shoes look like clogs but they're made out of leather and he stomps up the steps in them. Under his trouser legs I can see his ankles, through his thin socks they look like fists, and his legs, wide and bow-shaped, are seaman's legs. Big buttocks. And a back so wide that it stretches his jacket tight. And his hair. Although it's shorter than in Paris, it's still so long and thick that the curls on the back of his neck swing with every step.

At the door, he looks back for a moment. 'Here?'

'Yes, there.'

He switches over his bag to his left hand to open the door. I myself am carrying two suitcases and have to hold them firmly away from me to give him space. In my room he turns around a few times. He sees the canvases on the wall, he spots the bed, the dressing table, the window; he thinks that this is his room. 'That door there, it's in there,' I say.

Once in his own room he immediately sits on the bed. Just a moment ago, he was looking all around him, but here he has no interest in the paintings on the wall. I was proud of them, but the effect is indeed different now, on this autumn morning the canvases are actually not remarkable. Maybe Gauguin is just getting a feel for the atmosphere in the room. That's the most important thing anyway.

'Don't you mind that I have to go through your room every time I want to go downstairs?' he says.

'That's no problem at all.'

His trunk, which arrived a few days ago, is waiting for him in the corner.

'I thought this morning: maybe I should have written to tell you when precisely I would come, but you have already prepared everything,' he says.

'Then, in any case, I could have picked you up from the station.'

'Much too early, good that I didn't do that.' Now he walks round each wall and looks at what I've made. 'The Sunflowers'. 'The Night Café'. 'The Bedroom'. He nods, but says nothing. He wipes his hands and lets himself fall onto the bed as if to test its firmness, then immediately relaxes.

'It's a new bed,' I say.

Lying there, his body looks like a large, strong dog.

'I'll let you rest for a bit,' I say.

'I'd like that, my friend.'

With his hands behind his head, he quickly looks around the room and gives me a lopsided smile, as if to say that it's not bad at all.

When I close the door of my own room behind me, I can see the little square in a sombre light through the window. The shrubs in the rain. It's good that he can now, in his room, see my painting of this house which I've made so yellow and so blue. That's how it looks when it's sunny. Because he has to know that he's really in the South. The small yellow house in the sun on a square – that's how I imagined it, wasn't it? – with a studio downstairs where we stand side by side, painting, one canvas after another. Yes. That's how I imagine it. But also in my mind the feeling resonates more and more that it's all worthless, far too hurried, crazy lines in which no one sees anything, apart from me when I'm drunk or elated. And I'm so sure of that because Gauguin walks around here and will become the norm. And while we work like that, side by side, his big head will get overcome by boredom, he'll stay just for lack of something better and brood on how to get out.

This rain is not good for me, it's very bad luck. Just now when I'm becoming a bit feverish. But Gauguin has

34

come and is lying in his bedroom resting. In three months, a few weeks, tomorrow, at this moment, he is the leader of the studio.

And yet, it's a beautiful little house.

That evening we sit in the crowded café. First we looked for a place at the back, but then walked back to an empty table by the window. *Vincent has a guest. A painter too. That's where he belongs then: the art world.* We are both tired, but we talk about Gauguin's life in Brittany.

'You should've seen it, they were walking around everywhere, the painters. From every door that opened, out staggered one of those foolish braggarts. Every street corner that you turned: there's another one of those clowns. Forever painting, painting, making average paintings and then rambling on about them. And to think that Jesus died for them as well...'

He's sitting, his legs wide, in front of me at the table, with his back towards the window that frames him. His eyes are clear and quick, and his boat-like jaw swivels to and fro as he watches the café behind me, talking continuously. A boxer, a fencer, a revolutionary, a puppeteer, an aviator. Red cheeks; his whole head is brown-red. This afternoon he told me he liked to be 'nice and warm'. He has a strong stomach, he has eaten maybe three times the amount I have.

'But not Bernard, right?' I say. 'He is serious. I was hoping you'd bring something from him.'

'Yes, yes, yes,' says Gauguin, 'he makes serious things. Bernard... Laval... and me. The rest is overpopulation.' Now it is clearly time to say something about me, but he just throws me a glance. Behind me Gauguin sees the people of Arles at the tables. It is noisy and busy and people are walking to and fro, but still this café always has a peaceful atmosphere: the clock in the middle above the bar, the tables against the walls where groups of people sit any old way with the same green water bottles always

35

placed on each one, and which are always served all at the same time. When it's empty this café is ordered and symmetrical; now people are swarming around the tables. Later I have to point out the regulars to Gauguin.

'You have to be here on time,' I say. 'If you come too late there's nothing left, and if you're too early you have to wait. But it is cheap. Cheap and good.' I am the host, I have to play the role of Gauguin's host in this café, but of course he also sees that all of these people have nothing to do with me. And how rigidly I sit here next to all of these lively folks who are hugging each other or bursting out laughing and drinking out of each other's glasses or slapping faces or bottoms, slap, slap, slap.

We have fresh glasses of cognac. I don't want to talk. I do want to talk, yes, but tomorrow. Now I would like to make a plan together. We're going to work tomorrow. The Crau? In the city? Over the coming days, there are so many places we'll need to visit to do some work. Gauguin wants to go to a bull fight. Also good. If we want to take advantage of the autumn, the colours, then we'll have to work flat out during the next five days. During the day outdoors, and in the evenings with the lights on inside.

Gauguin is slouching in his chair; his eyes are a bit droopy. Fine, I don't like being watched. It's so stuffy in here. What's the time?

Gauguin nods, to himself. 'Vincent,' he says.

Tomorrow. First sleep, begin tomorrow.

'Those sunflowers,' he says.

He hasn't let on before that he has noticed the paintings I made for his room. His moustache shimmers. His eyes too, from tiredness and cognac.

'Those sunflowers of yours,' he says. 'Those are more real than sunflowers.'

'Thank you.' I'm too tired to return the compliment. I wanted to make them so yellow, the yellow from here, but it's night time now and everything is like everywhere else.

We go home. When we get to my room he walks on to his.

'Good night,' I say.

He turns around and replies: 'The best of nights.' A bit later I hear him blow his nose for a long time, but then I realise it's him snoring and that, warm and satisfied, he has fallen asleep as soon as he climbed between the sheets.

He's been here for less than a week. I've been trying to lay on all of my charm, all through spring, summer and autumn; but ah, I have no charm, they all see me as some kind of dog, they don't want me to paint them, but him, he's already managed to woo Marie Ginoux. For both of us, he says. She even asked how she should dress.

But how long can it take to pick her up for heaven's sake? It is five, six, seven steps away from here. The door of the café is already open, you look inside, all right, you walk to the back, past the pool table, the tables along the wall, but that's ten, twelve, twenty steps, and there you ask Joseph if his wife is ready, and all right, first a drink, the woman must keep you waiting for a while, another drink, by now everyone else must also know what's about to happen, all the men and women in the Café de la Gare.

Gauguin, Marie? You're going to paint her? Next door? At the Dutchman's? This Dutchman, ah, what can we say... better to say nothing. But Mr Gauguin, yes, we know you, we've heard a lot about you, who doesn't know you, you're world famous, such a celebrity in our midst, how do you like Arles? A modest town, but with a lot of beauty, don't you think? Beauty or beauties? Both!

But then they can finally leave, can't they? Then they can just stand up and walk away, they don't have to wait until it's dark, do they? Marie has already shown that she's a lady by keeping everyone waiting. Joseph has given her some last-minute instructions – be back before six, don't make any new appointments, tell me everything that happens, don't take anything off, if something should happen anyway, leave immediately, in any case, I'll come and check up on you every half-hour. The working men and the gentlemen of the town, the Benoîts and the Michels, now also want her to go, the anticipation has lasted long enough, now just let it happen and we'll see what comes of it. And yes, finally, there comes Marie, almost solemnly walking past the tables. Gauguin stands up, she nods, he bows and offers her his arm and then, then they're finally on their way. My God, they look like a bride and groom.

But, still, I don't see them approaching. A pale sky hangs over the square; it makes everything look pretty. The shrubs in the square look wilted, dishevelled. I feel like painting. I can't wait.

All right, then I'll tidy up first. I'll make a tidy studio out of this. I've began to lift up the easel, but of course it will stay where it is, because at the easel we painters are in charge, sir. That's where it happens. And quickly put this chair and the field easel against the wall. Put the caps on the paint tubes and throw the empty tubes away. I'll put the jute in the shed, the whole roll and the parts we've cut out of it. The fibres creep up into your nose. I sneeze. I sneeze. I sneeze. The canvases on the wall, the Japanese prints, she'll like them.

They arrive. Gauguin opens the door and strides in with Marie on his arm. She's entirely in black, the attire of Arles, that's how she wants to be painted by Gauguin and she gives me a quick nod.

'Yes,' says Gauguin, 'a real Arlésienne, we can be proud, Vincent,' and at once he starts moving the table and the chairs around.

She reminds me of my mother, the way she passes her eyes across the corners of the room and then waits with an ambiguous smile. But otherwise she looks nothing like her. She's wearing a black jacket with feathers, a black skirt and a Prussian blue undershirt – she looks like she's been cut out of charcoal, but then with a light and soft and pensive face.

She doesn't speak. She lets Gauguin lead her to a chair, she lays the gloves she had been carrying in her left hand onto the table in front of her. Her movements are so measured and her figure so sharply outlined in space that she

40

must be feeling uncomfortable, naked. I want to reassure her, but she doesn't look at me.

Gauguin sets up a drawing. That sentence is short, but that's how long it takes him. He draws with coal, indolently, with the movements of someone who's interested in nothing. He has put a small pillow under his arse. With grey chalk, thin lines, begin at the beginning. And then elaborate with charcoal. A person isn't a landscape. I paint differently, more naturally.

I make it just as it is. The table in front. Yellow. Green. Hair. Nose. The figure. The table. Yellow wall. Her face will be grey. It's not that beautiful, but I keep the grey. The grey with lemon-yellow.

Pale lemon. Her face grey, the clothes black, black, black, with perfect pure raw Prussian blue. She's leaning against the green table and sits in a chair of orange wood.

There's a fellow standing outside, looking through the window. If I had an eye above my ear, in my hair, I'd be looking straight at him. I don't look over my shoulder. But after a while I look anyway. It's a small man like Michel, the would-be henchman who went after the Italians. He's sniggering.

Marie pulls her mouth into a smile.

This jute, you can't paint on it with a brush. You have to fling the paint on with a flick of the wrist and then push it out to the sides. That's what those people see me do now, that's how you paint. More people have come to the window, how many are standing there now? A group, a dark group. Someone taps on the window. Someone shouts something.

'They're calling you,' Gauguin says.

I know that. But I don't look, and then the same thing happens as with a child afraid of the dark: the entire invisible infinity rubs itself up against your back and you have to fight against it.

Marie must be feeling uncomfortable with these people looking at her, she's smiling a lot and now turns her face completely to Gauguin. I see how her body tenses up and slowly moves, following her face, slowly – it must take her a lot of effort. All right, all right, all right, I'll paint you like that, you just keep looking at him, then I'll paint you like that.

To me she has always said: 'No. Not now. I'm not a model. I don't want to. Ask someone else.' Or: 'Just ask one of the girls, ask Rachel, she'd sit with her pussy laid bare, I'm sure.'

'No, no,' I replied, 'not nude.' But it was pointless.

'No,' she said, 'no, sir, you would first have to have a bath, glue your mouth shut, cover your eyes, and even then I still wouldn't do it, because you're crazy.'

But Gauguin she found interesting.

She's sitting turned entirely towards him now. She's looking at him. Marie, you're a sort of sister to me, it's beautiful just like that, from the side, not fully in profile, I paint you like this. I adjust the figure, your face. You look intently at nothing.

At first, I would have wanted to make the yellow in the background even more yellow, but this light, lemon yellow, a bit pale, that is better. It would have been too sunny and too warm, and your world is not warm and maybe you take on the coldness of the world, but you have a good face and a good heart. There is so much affinity between us. That's why you sometimes have to tease me so sharply or exasperate me, like brothers and sisters do, because the affinity is also exasperating.

And your parasol on the table. And your gloves. Done.

I put my things down. I turn my head. The people in front of the window have disappeared. The little bit of colour the sky had today, has dissolved. Lifted up. The small square looks as if it's rolling towards our house because of the whirling dust and rubbish.

I walk over to Gauguin, look at what he's done. Now, is that all? Is that all? A sketch, not bad, but not more than a sketch. Humming, he puts down a few final lines; he looks

42

like a crone doing embroidery. Then, he too gathers his things and that's Marie's cue to stand up stiffly. She shuffles to Gauguin's easel to have a look.

'Now,' she says, 'now, it's me, it's really me, but you have flattered me, sir.'

'Not at all,' Gauguin says.

'Do I really look so mysterious?'

'A lady like you always has secrets.'

'All kinds of secrets.'

'That's right, milady.'

He offers her his arm and looks at me for a moment. 'I am very satisfied.'

After he's taken her back, we're both silent. Gauguin cooks and I compliment him on the food. He doesn't think it that special, but it makes me happy to eat a simple meal like this together in our house. We don't talk about the work that we have done this afternoon. I fear that I can only be honest and offend him. And I think about how I painted as if in a dream and how I actually wanted Marie to see how I work, and how that didn't happen.

Gauguin looks at my work for a moment and says, shortly: 'Bon.'

It is a fantasy. The studio was a fantasy, I could only walk around fantasising about it, but now it's become reality. Now it's become this. When I arrived here and saw Arles in the sun and had to squint, then I thought: now it's begun. I walked around like that, I saw budding and sprouting everywhere, the most delicate and colourful blossoms – blossoms and colours different from the past. And people who simply said hello as I passed them. The houses, not pretty, but friendly. Children who were just curious. I walked through the streets with my bag on my back and I had the sensation that I, through the solid feel of the trodden sand under my feet, and the expressions of the people, and the simple door of the boarding house which opened, that I, because all of that, was being accepted into the order of Arles. Of the South.

Now it's become this. Gauguin doesn't want this at all. We eat our food and drink the wine. Tonight we will drink more. Maybe we'll go for a walk, maybe we will pay a visit to the women. Gauguin looks tired and I probably do too. Let us talk quietly. I bring up Delacroix's Tasso print.

'I don't know it,' says Gauguin.

'You've seen it. Tasso in the institution.'

'Really I haven't.'

'You saw it in Paris, I'm sure of it.'

'I'm sure I haven't.'

I describe the print to him. The crowd before the cell windows, people sticking arms through the bars to prod and scoff at the poet and to snatch his manuscripts. And the gazing madness in Tasso's eyes, who's turning away and covering his body with a cloth or some fabric. Delacroix rendered Tasso in such a way that he is simultaneously ignoring and answering the people in front of the bars. It is a magnificent print. I say I'll arrange for Theo to send it to him.

'Please,' says Gauguin, 'I'd quite like to look at it.'

'Then I'll do it. I'll write to him tonight.'

From now on we'll always eat like this. The two of us are now putting in the hard preliminary work, organisational and emotional. So that others can join us in our small house and our small studio. Indeed. All these painters that will come here. The painters will stand beside one another, working, or go outside with their easels, and continue later in the studio. Every brushstroke opens up a new world in these men, like curtains you pull open, curtain after curtain.

This is only the third evening that we're sitting in the café together, but I'm thinking to myself: Gauguin and I come here every evening, that's what we do. We've been working at the Alyschamps. I had to get used to it, he set up his easel a few hundred metres from me and we didn't speak to each other, but I got well underway, and so did he. Maybe that's exactly what our studio will be: you separate and then come back together to show your worth to each other. Maybe.

Joseph's come to sit with us. With me or with Gauguin? We've just finished eating, soup and bread, always soup and bread, and Joseph sweeps his hand over the small table. He looks pensive. I don't often see him this quiet. Gauguin talks about something, Joseph divides his attention between Gauguin's words and his own rubbing hand. I only half listen. Suddenly they look at me. Are they expecting an answer?

Apparently Gauguin has evoked the image of Paris and Agostina Segatori for Joseph. 'That café was called Le Tambourin,' he says. 'And the tables were what shape? Tambourines. And on the wall hung? Tambourines. Painted tambourines. Isn't that right, Vincent? And bouquets of flowers hung there as well. Painted flowers and bouquets. And among it all walked Agostina Segatori.'

Of course, Gauguin knows that café and, of course, he then also knows Agostina, I shouldn't be so surprised about that. But he knows more, otherwise he wouldn't start talking about it. He makes his voice sound dark when he says her name, 'Agostina', and directs his inquiring glance at me, as if he wants to pass the conversation over to me.

'Agostina?' says Joseph.

'A Neapolitan,' I say. Joseph gets what I mean.

'A real Neapolitan.' Tough. Smiley. Sad.

'And Vincent knows it because he played her tambourine,' Gauguin says. Joseph shakes his head and hisses from the corner of his mouth. We all see a hairy tambourine before us now, so obscene, I don't like it.

Joseph is wearing his beige suit again, which I thought was only for Sundays.

'Sorry, friend,' says Gauguin, 'I didn't want to say it like that, but you and Segatori, you were together, a couple. We all thought: that Vincent's done well for himself. If you can marry a woman with a successful café...' That last thing he says to Joseph... Then he gives me a pat on the arm and leans back.

What does he want? He's up to something, Gauguin.

'Was it a gypsy business?' Joseph says.

'No,' says Gauguin, 'not really. It was a business full of Luigis and Paolos and Ennios. At those round tambourine tables sat the entire Italian underworld of Paris, actually, forging her plans.'

'No, no,' I say, 'it wasn't that bad. Everyone thought so, but it's exaggerated.'

'When anything happened in Paris, a robbery, a raid, the police came to Le Tambourin to pick up the perpetrators,' Gauguin says. 'Agostina Segatori was the mother of the underworld. And you know that I don't like offending anyone, Vincent.'

'It's not true,' I say.

Gauguin looks at Joseph and me for a moment, as if he's weighing up the risk of the discussion, and then says: 'You are right, sergeant.' How in God's name am I meant to take that? *You are right, sergeant.*

'*La mère de la canaille,*' says Joseph. 'And you were the man at the top, surely.' He looks at Gauguin. 'Vincent really doesn't look like a *père.*'

'No, and it wasn't like that either,' I say. We're cracking jokes. Look, the wrinkles above Gauguin's nose, he's starting to focus on a game. And Joseph doesn't know how or what, but he feels that there's play of some sort going on, and he's giving it a try. What should I say? Agostina was a woman who wanted to help me. Maybe she herself didn't believe that the punters in her café were fit for me, but still she let me hang up some of my paintings and prints

46

on the walls. Even if I didn't get them all back. When I didn't have any money, I could pay a bill of twenty-three francs with a painting. 'Oh,' she said, 'oh, Vincent, but that's worth much more than twenty-three francs.' Black hair, black eyes with added sad leaden grey. She always wore coral necklaces, constantly made sure she had spectacular coloured accents in her clothes. Twenty years ago she must have been even prettier, all those stories must have been true, but then she didn't have that seriousness in her face, those sad cheeks. Her lips were often pressed together, as if she – indeed – secretly controlled things. In the beginning she came to sit at my table and asked me how things were going. She once cut my hair. With a pair of blunt scissors. She sat me down on a chair in the kitchen and sat herself down on my lap; she had to lift up her skirt, and like that, breathing over me, not talking, she helped me get rid of my messy hair. She swept away the loose hair from my head with her hands.

We're cracking jokes. Men like Gauguin and Joseph talk about these things in a teasing way, they try to get you riled up. But I feel ashamed, so terribly.

'Why are you not rich then,' Joseph says, 'if you were part of that world?'

'Who knows how rich I am, Joseph,' I say. I try to talk like a gentleman in a club. But they don't play along.

Gauguin waves his arm in the air. 'No, it's exactly the opposite, Vincent was more likely a victim of her ploys and her passions and her problematic friends. So I've heard, at least. Vincent, sergeant, correct me if I'm wrong.'

As if I've been lying and in danger of getting caught up in it, my mind works cautiously. Not cautious, scared. As if there's something to give away. Because Gauguin and Joseph are now looking at me in the same way as those Italians in Le Tambourin. I had had so much sympathy for them. Those Italians weren't liked in Paris, nor in other places, by the way, not in Arles either. They were in the doghouse, I told them that, but I sat with them at their table

47

and drank with them and enjoyed myself. We laughed at all sorts of things, at my paintings on those walls as well, but I understood. They gave me cognac and beer and Agostina Segatori would run her strong hand through my hair. And then one day, suddenly, they surrounded me, the Italians of Le Tambourin, and started shouting 'Thief!' 'That's theft, Vincent,' they said. 'You've given them away, so if you now take those paintings with you, it will be theft, sir. Or are you trying to say that we are thieves?'

Ennio was doing the talking, but the whole clique was there, they'd shoved two or three tables together and had the café to themselves. 'A misunderstanding, Vincent. We're not thieves. You gave them to Agostina yourself.'

'No,' I said, 'some I did, those ones with the flowers I gave to Agostina as a present, but these other ones, no.'

'Agostina!' Ennio shouted towards the back. 'Is it true, those paintings were a present, right? Or are you saying that Agostina is lying?' He now came at me to push me towards the door.

Agostina was in the kitchen, you could hear her move. 'Yes,' she shouted, 'presents, gifts!'

What else could she do? She wasn't free, Agostina, what should she have done? She didn't have any money, she had a lot of expenses, and of course her health was bad and she was always working, until late into the night. She was forced to, due to poverty, for health reasons. I came with a wheelbarrow to take my paintings back. Pranzini and all of his kind stood around me in a circle, blocking me in, but I just took what was mine. If they were planning on grabbing me by the arms or trying to push me, that was their business, I was going to leave with my canvases. But it didn't happen like that. The aggression was much more ruthless. Pranzini came up closer and closer to me. I felt his moustache against my cheek, as if he were kissing me; it confused me so much that I froze. *This was aggression.* From that moment on bursts of anxiety kept shooting through my chest. There was another one, Prado, who also stood in front of me. Pranzini, breathing in my face, balancing on his toes. Prado, loitering, observing; he wasn't looking at me. In his buttoned-up jacket, his tight collar, the cuffs, the rings and the shiny shoes, he looked like a nobleman. He was taller than Pranzini and – I only realise this now – his face was dull and colourless, like a reflection in a window pane. He was not threatening, but that might have been precisely what was alarming: sooner or later he would have to intervene and you had no idea what kind of force he would use.

I ran away.

I was ashamed, so terribly. It's that damned shame that's always scorching me. Now as well. Because I don't know what game Gauguin and Joseph are playing, again I'm not part of everything and everyone. Breath comes juddering out of my mouth – a sign of shame. My hot head, the sweat in my hair, my burning eyes, shame, shame, shame.

'Friend,' Gauguin says, 'I've heard what happened, Mr Vincent was grabbed at either end and given a beating. I've heard about it, of course it had been planned in advance, that's right, isn't it, Vincent?' And to Joseph: 'It's a different kind of café from this one.'

From whom did he hear this? Lautrec or Bernard or one of the others. Maybe from Theo? Theo wouldn't say it like that: *at either end.*

'It was a misunderstanding,' I say. 'I had hung up some paintings in the café, like an exhibition. But there were some people who thought that Agostina had been given them or bought them. And those were certainly not honest fellows. But later it was all sorted out.'

'Sorted out? Blood was flowing, Vincent,' says Gauguin. 'Theo had to stem it with his own handkerchief.'

'And that's why you left Paris,' Joseph says. 'I would've too. The ground got too hot under your feet.' He seems so benign with those thin eyelashes.

Gauguin laughs. A monotonous laugh, his voice has become nasal now that we've had so much to drink.

'Monsieur Joseph, could we have some more cognac, please?'

Joseph walks to the bar. He's been standing all this time, I thought he had come to sit at our table but maybe he just stopped for a short time out of politeness when he came to bring us a bottle or some glasses. I'm ashamed, because Agostina doubtlessly makes him think of Marie. Gives him the idea that Marie and I have, I don't know, a connection, that I've had her on my lap. That's out of the question, not in a million years, and yet Marie and Agostina do seem alike – the hope and the warmth I feel, as well as the disappointment.

December 1888

Gauguin is cooking in our small house. He's put a pot with vegetables on the stove and is baking meat in the frying pan, which has more than paid for itself. We now eat at home and not in the café; every day we save two francs. This is often a nice moment. Gauguin showing his skills. He used to be a ship's cook. But the mood is stormy. The gas lamp is on. I've been trying to write a letter to Theo all evening, but Gauguin is working again. With his warm leather boots on, the taste of food and wine still in his mouth. Because then I don't talk. Humming, he's rubbing his brushes clean. I cannot pin down my thoughts for the letter like this. We now work inside every day and I could not wish for anything more than to go outdoors. *You can, can't you? I'm not holding you back.* I could go out now and paint the night clouds, but he'd notice. *Vincent is going outside.* He does take notice, has his opinion and talks to his friends about it. What does he write in his letters? What do Bernard and all the others think about what's going on here?

I don't want to argue. To everything I say, Gauguin says: 'You are right, sergeant.'

The gleam of the gas lamp sweeps through the space, light and dark mix with each other, the illusions of the day and the illusions of the night. Gauguin is stirring. He's tossed the paint-cloth he uses to move the pans over his shoulder. The spoons are in a pot. Gauguin is so productive, in any case, that's what his stay here has delivered. Because of the regularity. Because of the discipline. But I can barely move because of it. Gauguin sees everything.

I'm going to read to him about Prado from the newspapers.

Every day, we read to each other from *L'Intransigeant*, about the court case against Prado, the murderer of the whore, La Crevette. Every day, there's a new episode that interests and amuses us both. I wouldn't want to say that I know him, Prado; even if I did see him in Le Tambourin, I don't know him at all, but to everything I read about him I add the frightening, yes, ghastly impression he left on me in Paris. In the court he keeps presenting himself as a different person, his pleas always boil down to the same thing: *je suis pas ce qui je suis*. He cannot be the murderer because he is Prado, the stockbroker in Paris. No, he is the illegitimate son of Napoleon the Third and a lady-in-waiting. No, he is a writer, a journalist, he ghost-writes Zola's stories. He is Prado, the son-in-law of the President of Mexico. He will write his memoirs. Everyone lets themselves be deceived. Gauguin still can't decide which version of Prado he adores the most. I thought it would be the jungle warrior from Lima, Gauguin could see himself in that too, but no, he likes 'the honourable' even more, the Madrilenian nobleman with his estate and his noble obligations. 'My country estate is calling me,' he says and Gauguin whistles through his teeth in admiration. That a murderer can so slyly disappear from the scene... He often re-enacts Prado's roles, with a cloth tied around his head, with the posh accent of the noble Prado, or with the sharp questions Prado uses to drive his opponents, the accusing witnesses, up the wall in despair.

I open the newspaper, looking for a piece about Prado. A few days ago he was convicted, the guillotine. He laughed about it. He sat in his death cell and said: 'A man like me doesn't die on the scaffold.'

'He wants to escape!' the journalists said immediately, 'he has a plan!' Gauguin thinks so too, but I don't believe it. These last few days Prado's demeanour has changed. I read aloud. Gauguin is standing, legs straight, stirring the pot; it looks like he isn't enjoying it, but that's just a pretence. If I start reading now, he might suddenly raise his head and spread his arms and start playing one of

Prado's roles: 'My country estate!' he shouts, and he whirls through our house.

'Listen,' I say. *L'affaire Prado. L'assassin Prado, until recently so full of bravura, now seems defeated and without hope. He sits in his cell, writing hour after hour, but often he stops, pen in his hand, staring into space, as a tear rolls down his cheek.'*

Gauguin has now turned around and comes to sit at the table. Slightly bent forward, his chair sideways, his eyes on the paper, he sits in the same position as me and everything I read out now takes on extra meaning between us.

'"If I must die," Prado appears to be thinking. He is writing the story of his life, and has asked a priest, monsieur Beauquesne, to take over his work "when I have sailed across the Styx in his boat".'

Gauguin is now a gondolier, moving an imaginary oar, and glides through the kitchen, but soon stops again.

'Earlier Prado expressed regret for his deeds and talked about how things could have been different now that he has a child, and that the cradle of that child could have formed the boundary between good and evil. "I feel guided towards a new path." But it is too late.'

It is true. It moves me. It is childish, but that's how it goes. Regret at the end of your life, the black realisation that this could not have been prevented. Prado must have known this, he did know it and he closed his eyes in the face of it and just went on. The convulsing remorse and the shame.

But Gauguin says: 'Let him just kick the bucket then. It's no fun this way. He has to go through with it. "A man like me doesn't die on the scaffold!" No backtracking and whining in your cell now.' With a whisk he puts the food on the table, on top of the newspaper.

'No,' I say, 'everything has changed for him, don't you understand?' He is being condemned, he will die. The reaping is done, that is clear, but now it has come to what he has sown.

But I don't say this aloud, because Gauguin would answer: 'You are right, sergeant.' I will tell him later, when he wants to go to sleep, then I will scream it into his ears.

We sit like that and eat and drink, until we've fallen into silence again.

'The married couple Gauguin-Van Gogh at the table,' says Gauguin, 'after forty years of marriage.'

Anything I say will lead to a discussion. I don't want that. Then I say: 'I saw Prado, in Le Tambourin in Paris. With Pranzini.'

Gauguin immediately leaps on my words. 'Tell me, go on, tell!' His spitefulness has completely disappeared. If it were possible he would haul the story out of my memory himself. He wants to know everything. 'Did he sit with his elbow on the table? Was he watching the door? Did he smoke? Did he whisper? No, of course not, surely he sat broadcasting his affairs to everyone at the top of his voice. Prado and Pranzini, two peas in a pod!'

'I don't know about that,' I say. 'I'm also not sure if I ever actually saw him, but they did go there, to Le Tambourin. It could be, that's what I mean. It's possible that I have seen him.'

'Possible!' Gauguin isn't planning on taking that into account. 'Tell me, what did they talk about?' He'd prefer it if I made something up, if I served up some nonsense. 'What did they discuss? His estate in Spain? Pranzini!'

Gauguin springs to his feet and moments later returns with a razor. 'My name is Pranzini,' he shouts and makes cutting movements in the air. He's a strong fellow, but due to his stocky build he can sometimes give the impression of a dwarf, Gauguin, the burlesque scoundrel, and Pranzini, who with his razor blade snuffed the lives out of dozens of people in a flash.

Why have I started talking about this? This is how you get entangled in lies. I don't tell him anything else. But Gauguin already seems satisfied; a game, he can play another game. He is not who he is. He puts on a mask and from behind it he can do what he wants.

This irritates me so much. The way he talks about Prado, it's been driving me up the wall all evening. That man now realises that it's all been for nothing, that it now comes down to a higher plan, about the role he will play in the grand story of God. Yes. The intention that He had for him. Like a seed. What comes out of that seed?

How he chased me out of Paris. That's how it is. That's how it seems, right?

Shut up. Quiet. I want to think about this. Wait. I'm going outside, I'm going away for a bit, maybe I'll storm out of the door, a bit oddly and unexpectedly, but by now Gauguin's used to it. Outside I walk into the night. The air is heavy, I sniff for the freshness, but it's not here. Maybe there. Maybe higher. Or higher, that's nonsense, I'm just standing in the square, but at least there's space here.

The thought of Prado, who ends lives. So clear. He cuts throats. Deaths, unmistakable deaths. Like furrows in the ground. What comes of it? I have a clear idea, as if it really happened, of Prado in Paris. In a street in Montmartre. Outside Le Tambourin, but in a quiet, spacious street, just like now, dark and fresh. How he took me by the elbow and turned his brown-eyed face towards me and said: 'They don't want you here.' He had on a thick jacket, he needed it in this cold. He said, calmly: 'This is no place for you. Everyone knows that. You are the only one blind to it. But not any more. You think that we're all crazy. You're going to leave and we never want to see you again.'

'No.'

'Otherwise I will cut your throat. And that of your dear brother.'

I was already running away. Prado wanted to push me but I was already running, it looked as if he was sending me strength with his outstretched arms.

I don't feel like going back inside any more. The moon is in the sky, so round and big, a gong which will someday be struck. I walk around the city. The city where I live. Gauguin will soon leave. He is vague about it because he might not want to make me angry, but I have the idea that he's been talking about it with the others, with Joseph and Roulin and everyone. *Think of us for a second, Mr Gauguin, we are, after all, immortalised by you; well now, not we ourselves, but our city. Our place in the world, I would say; now people in Paris can see it. Ah, and we've had so much sympathy for you! We walked past that house and we saw you sitting at the table together and we thought: we're lucky we don't have to join in. Not because of you, of course!*

And all those others, those other painters, have you told them not to come? Marie here, Marie was a bit scared of it, but no one took your friend's ideas seriously – oh well, your friend. We would have welcomed them, definitely! But we had no illusions. Maybe for a while, for a moment, when you came. With you we saw immediately that some serious painting would be done.

They haven't arrived, they never will. Never. Because Gauguin's told them God knows what. Do you think he invited people over, suggested that they come, presented a positive image, said something favourable? Bernard, Toulouse, everyone in Paris... Has he taught me anything? No! Yes, but not what I wanted to learn. I can reproach him for so many things, lay so many things at his door, but I already feel myself falling through, my breath becomes hard to swallow, my ears start ringing as I sink backwards into the realisation that it would never work, the studio, the painters, the friendship. It would never, ever, work.

This is how I have to describe it to Theo: a raft made of branches that falls apart under me. I don't reproach anyone for anything. Not Gauguin. Mr Gauguin, his soul is not here. His body, sure, and his filled stomach and his eyes

56

that see everything and his warm feet, but his heart wanders elsewhere over the earth.

We calmly walk to the brothel. Calmly, distantly. The wind has subsided, but still all the passers-by walk with their shoulders hunched. Gauguin too.

The gatekeeper at the Bout d'Arles nods at us. The salon is a large hall and we always have to give our eyes a bit of time to get used to it. The bare walls are painted in blue plaster; some fifty men, citizens and Zoauves, sit at small tables, like in a classroom. And the women walk around in sapphire blue and crimson and emerald and bright yellow gowns; here, there is no restraint. You expect the space to have the acoustics of a station hall, but no, it's snug, and once we sit down we can follow all the conversations. People are talking about the murder of the Zoauves and about Prado. Gauguin immediately starts his performance. He strolls up and down through the salon, from the couch to the door and back again. Then he stands in the middle and spins round on his heels with his arms spread out. The moment everyone is looking at him he roars and moves his arm forward as if he's stabbing someone with a sword, and another time, one more stab, and he says, with extra calmness in his voice: 'If you would please excuse me, my estate is calling me.'

Everyone knows exactly what that's about, everyone understands the joke, Gauguin is pretending Prado is the murderer of the Zoauves. Everyone is also very drunk.

I have, of course, also noticed the women. Rachel is here. And this time she does allow it. Now she's treating me like the other men, a nod without a glance as a sign that we can choose her.

I choose her.

Rachel. I walk along with her.

She looks almost Japanese, with her pale skin. Her eyes, of course, are bigger and the stooped posture with which she walks is not due to modesty but dislike, perhaps. Disgust. She has often expressed her loathing and rejected me as vehemently as possible; now she is quietly walking in front of me. She is tough. She looks like she's been fighting her way out of arguments for ever. She isn't as pretty as some Arlésiennes. Her brown hair hangs in curls that look so vibrant; I can imagine how they feel as they glide over your forehead.

The little room she takes me to is bare. The wall behind the bed is covered in floral-print wallpaper. A bed with a quilt. Grey stains on the wooden floor. A jug of water on the little table. I feel like drinking that water. In two of the corners hang oil lamps which need to be refilled, their flames are small and spread a blue light along the walls. Me and Rachel. She's the one to make a move. From the front she looks like she doesn't have any bones, but she turns around as she takes off her clothes and I see her shoulder-blades move under her flesh. Add ten years to it, ten years of atrophy and you have Sien. But she is not Sien yet, and the sight of her white back makes me wild with desire.

She's gone to lie down on the bed. I've stuck my penis into her. Rachel breathes through her mouth. Our bellies meet. I move. I look at her curls. I actually want to ask her how other men do it, but no. Her curls. They're an ashy colour, it's not a flattering thing to say but it's true, and they are so big and almost completely round, so wonderful. They are lying still on the cushion. I'm afraid that if I blow, they'll stay motionless. Rachel must have pulled the hairpins out of her hair, because when we were walking upstairs her curls were pinned up and more compacted. I move. I have to hold back because otherwise it will all be over straight away, and in that moment of a standstill my thoughts start wandering.

In the room next to us Gauguin is lying now, probably also with his penis in that woman. I'm imagining how we sat arguing at the dinner table this evening and I imagine that same Gauguin is now next door fucking and spreading his seed. I imagine not only Gauguin's bare back on a woman on a bed in a room – I see every room in this house separately, with separate oil lamps that throw their patchy light across a bed in which two people are copulating, the woman underneath and on top a man from the salon, the gentleman from the bakers, I see Roulin rocking back and forth on a woman, Benoît whimpering and slaving away, and I see Milliet, Milliet with Rachel.

He talks to her as he's inside her and they look smilingly at each other. That's how lovely it can be between a man and a woman. That's how Milliet's last night must have gone, before he left for Indochina.

I do want to ask Rachel about it. I do want to talk to her about Milliet, I will say that I miss him too, *he was what kept me going.*

Milliet is now fighting in the heat. With his comrades, even when shooting and marching, he probably cannot hold back and suddenly allows a grin to appear on his face. I do want to talk about the fly-covered dog we painted, or whatever it was, I've forgotten exactly what it was. And that, of course, is not a suitable topic.

'Isn't it working?' she says. 'Come, I'll do it,' and she raises herself up on her elbows.

'No,' I say, 'this, it's good like this.' Oh, Rachel. Her body is so sultry, I feel as dizzy as one time when I spend the entire day standing in the burning sun and I want to sink into her entirely, into her sweating body and into her cunt.

This helps me to paint, to paint people. I have to, as it were, paint her innermost parts, and by innermost I mean her vagina, the walls of her vagina with which she now feels me and which I now feel. I imagine that my penis fills her so much that I see it move back inside her body as I look at her.

'Go on then,' Rachel says.

Do I hear Gauguin shouting? It's echoes that I hear, there's a racket downstairs. Someone is shouting, there's shouting, but that could be anyone. It's all of those men who have come.

'Vincent!' It sounds like my name. Somewhere in the hallways. Or is it an argument? Is something happening? Maybe someone is getting stabbed again.

Rachel pushes my head aside with her fingertips. I lie staring at her; all this time, she is simply doing her job.

Maybe Gauguin's already finished. Maybe he's already gone downstairs and is talking to someone. I think so. Maybe that's what I heard. Do I hear him shouting again? 'Vincent!' Somewhere in this house someone, something, someone is shouting my name, 'Vincent!', but I'm still here. 'Vincent! The estate is calling!' It seems as if there's a whole following behind Gauguin now, marching through the narrow hallways, up the stairs. 'Vincent!' Hammering on doors. On this door? 'Vincent!' I have to shout something back that he should shut up, but I cannot.

'You're not really a joking type, huh?' Rachel says.

'No,' I say.

There's a party downstairs, they're singing and making a mess. If only it were quiet. Rachel now lays her hand on my shoulder. That shoulder is probably a bit clammy now, she's stroking it with her nails and that feels wonderful, almost refreshing.

She just has to endure this. Of course she'd rather do it with another. How does he do it, I want to ask. I was thinking this moments ago. Do you know Milliet? Do you know Gauguin? Do you know Joseph? And Benoît. Milliet she knows for sure, that I know, Milliet's had her, just like he's probably had every other girl in Arles. Oh, Rachel. Why are you permitting this now, you've thrown me out before, you've taken my money, and now...

Wait.

Wait.

Wait.

Wait.

Wait.

60

She's quietly getting dressed now. Her gown. She puts pins in her hair. She puts her make-up on. I sit on the bed. I thought for a moment that it was already time to leave, but she starts talking again. 'I don't feel like going downstairs,' she says.

'Me neither,' I say.

We're sitting here, in hiding, each in our own way. It is difficult, the most difficult thing there is, to start a new life. I want to say that to her, because she's sitting there thinking up ways out and fantasising about where she could go. It's the most difficult thing there is, but you might succeed. That's what I want to say, but she doesn't look at me.

'What is it?' I ask.

'Nothing,' she says, 'nothing, what would it be?' She stands up and walks to the door and as soon as she opens it we hear Gauguin and the others singing and shouting. She's gone.

My body feels heavy, relaxed, and I don't feel like moving. I can stay sitting here, maybe I can sleep in this bed and leave in the morning. But then Rachel suddenly pops her head around the door. Irritated. She steps inside, turns the lamp off. 'Allez,' she says and lets me pass before closing the door.

You come up with something and then you do it and then so many consequences and events unfold that the connection between them gets lost. Lost, that's exactly what it is. I remember the boy, that boy walking there with his too-tight clothes and his recently cut hair, who shyly turns his head away from me. A week ago, he and a bunch of others followed me through Montmajour Avenue, thwack, throwing stones. At my back, my head, the things I was carrying on my back. Thwack! I never react to these things, but this time I thought I had to defend myself. There was a rock in my bag and I took it in my hand, turned around and hurled it at the boy's head. My target was his cheek but, now that he had been hit, I was shocked: blood, a gushing slash. He dropped to the floor and I was scared he was going to be permanently scarred. But now I see that there was nothing wrong with him, just a bit of anxiety now that he was not with the others. But the others, of course, are still around, and this boy in their company will, at some point, catch up with me and then maybe I will be the one who should be scared.

Why?

Where am I walking to? It will dawn on me any second now. Something will appear familiar. There, the small brothel, and behind it the big one. That'll be it. I knock. The owner opens the door. The man, whose eyes keep darting around, stares at me. He wipes his hands off with a cloth and says nothing, standing in the doorway with his legs wide apart, not intending to let me through. 'Is Rachel there?' I say.

'Rachel?' After a moment he goes inside. I just stand waiting at the door.

Then she arrives. 'Yes?' she says. 'Yes?' Behind her in the hallway there are people peering over each other's shoulders.

I've no idea what I should say. Rachel's hair is pinned up, the curls winding their way upwards. It looks as if flax or felt has accumulated on her hair. Her face is pale and her mouth is open as if I've caught her by surprise and she will now tell me the truth. 'Is that for me?' she asks.

'Here,' I say and I give her the handkerchief.

She holds out her hand, as if by reflex, but now, of course, she looks disgusted. There's a piece of ear in it. 'Look after it well,' I say. I had better leave again as soon as possible. I was actually looking for him. Maybe I wanted to say 'I've come for Gauguin', and then by accident said 'Rachel'.

I don't know.

Back.

I turn around one more time towards Rachel and say 'I'm going home', but the door has been shut.

I move forward very slowly now, waddling like a duck, but that comes from tiredness. Or from the stiffness of my body. I don't know any more, and yet my memory works perfectly. I still remember – I'm recalling it right now – the cleaning lady over there with the headscarf and the bag, shuffling across the pavement, there she is walking in front of me, who I once accompanied home. Accompanied. She didn't want me to, I remember that very clearly, but at the time I didn't realise it. She was a bit scared, but I wanted to tell her about the laundry she had with her, the posture she adopted when she was washing it, and the strength of her labour. 'Au secours!' she said. And screamed. Horrible.

Is it warm? No, cold. No, warm. Such pain. I've cut into my head, I still remember that clearly. I go back to my house to bind up the wound. And then to sleep. Maybe to the doctor's. Quickly, quickly. But – I – am – not – moving.

Where did I just come from? Gauguin? He wasn't there. Where is he? At home. On the train. At sea. Looking out. I imagine him like this: in a thick jacket, under swirling skies, sailing across the waves towards the tropics.

To have a friend. I'm sneaking away like a criminal, I can't stay standing up, straight and proud, I can't face the men who walk through the streets with their hands behind their backs and the women who are always together, arm in arm, hand in hand, deep in conversation, and that's why I'm moving so furtively. Oh! for a friend. My mother and my sister, they always walked side by side. With furrowed brows and frightened eyes, as a precaution. Fright in the eyes, so that they could immediately agree with father when he expressed his disapproval. Or comfort and support each other when father showed me the door.

I walk through the streets. Now and for ever since then. I walk through the streets by myself. And all these other people walk past me and if I talk, they get angry. I talk normally. I walk normally, I work normally. They laugh at me. I just try, I try. But people have lives together which I know nothing about. They all know what you have to do and what it means if you say this or that. I just talk and they get annoyed. Rachel has complained about me because I didn't want to leave her room. I don't understand, but yet it is so. That washerwoman ran away screaming. I don't understand, but yet it is so. I walk with Benoît and Michel to chase the Italians away, but that's not right, they chase after me.

Segatori on my lap.

Marie Ginoux.

Gauguin in his leather boots. *You are right, sergeant.*

Throwing stones, God damn it.

What I paint makes no sense to them. None.

Horrible, horrible shame.

I'm at the square by my house. The sky is the colour of limestone. It takes so long, I go so slowly I look like I'm falling down. Filthy raindrops lie on the dusty pavement. The door is open, thank God, I don't have to use the keys and find the handle and push – I stumble inside, I can go upstairs straight away. Stumble, stumble, up the stairs. Now that you don't have a suitcase in your hand, you can just walk. But oh. Such squalor. Blood. My God, everywhere. On the walls, the floor, I slip on it. My God. Yes. I did the cutting upstairs and then I plummeted down the stairs; first I stood at the top gathering my strength and then I let myself slide along the wall and tumbled halfway down. It's in my eyes too, the blood. I go downstairs, to get some cloths. There are no cloths. Newspapers, then. Grab them, just pile them up. Take them with you to the stairs to wipe everything off. Before someone comes in. Later someone will come inside and see all this mess. Wipe it off. The wall first or the stairs? On the steps you can barely see it, you just feel it. If I make sure no one goes upstairs. Tomorrow it'll be dry. But the walls. I wipe, but I just smear everything around.

Wait. First shut the door. I go down, down the steps, push against the door. Shut. It's opening again. What now? I push the door against the frame, softly, so that it stays there. I want to barricade the door. But I can't. There's only one thing I can still do. Lie down on the bed, first get up these endless stairs and then lie down. Yes.

JANUARY 1889

People, come. The entire square is flooded with people, still more coming in from the side streets. I don't have to climb up onto a platform, because a space has been kept free for me. People, you don't know what to expect and maybe I don't know what to say, but now that you're listening I will tell. Listen.

And look, there. All the nightingales. Swallows and owls and nightingales. It was so dark there, so dark. That was in Belgium, the Borinage. Icy cold. Then the beasts eat you up from inside out and then they come bringing soup, the filthiest soup you've ever seen in your life that crunches between your teeth. Over there! There they are, so many of them!

***

People, come. The entire square is flooded with people, still more coming in from the side streets. I don't often speak in front of such a crowd and that's why I ask in advance for patience and understanding. Because what I want to talk about here is quite simple, but due to my way of speaking perhaps still unclear.

There are three reasons why this world – the world we live in – is the best of all possible worlds. The first reason is that God has made this world. Out of all the possible worlds, he has chosen this one, out of all the possible elements and facets, he selected these.

The second reason is the presence of evil. You all recall Candide: so much misery, so much disaster, so much destruction and pain. It is true. There is gloom and loneliness and death, and they are there in overwhelming quantities, so much so that for some people they seem like all that there is. But this isn't all for anyone. That shows how good this world is.

The third reason is that this world is the only world. There is no alternative. Everything that happens is the best that can happen because nothing else happens.

I told you that there are three reasons, but that was a lie. There are hundreds and hundreds. I could analyse them all for you, one by one, but these three reasons are sufficient for you. I can repeat them; if you want I'll repeat them a hundred times, until you understand. These are the best reasons out of all the possible reasons.

*****

People, come. The square is full, everyone is standing around me. How to die? That's what I'll talk about, if you listen.

When a person dies, it becomes clear who he really is, what God's intention with him is. Then he is a link in the chain.

How do people die? The poor wretches go unnoticed, their candle doused. Rachel does notice it, she notices it every day because she keeps dying bit by bit until one day, there'll be nothing left of her. And Theo will be welcomed by jubilant angels, everything will fall away from him and he will float. Gauguin will freeze in mid-movement, freeze and harden immediately, fall down with a bang.

And myself. I don't know, but I'm so scared it will be the end of me in a place where I don't know anybody. Out of the way. Still, everything will finally fall into its place, like in a family. Father, mother, son, daughter, and they're also brother and sister, and the father has a brother and also his own father and mother. I will fall into such an order after death. That's what I've always believed.

Maybe it will turn out that I was of significance, however small, for other painters, purely by the fact that I persisted, that I worked. That's what I've always believed. Maybe in paintings by Gauguin or Bernard or whoever, there's an idea or a colour or something else – that they didn't reach for but that came to be through their standing next to me working for a while, or seeing one of my works. Something that will have made the group stronger. I will be a part of a pattern.

A father, a mother. A link in a chain.

That's what I've always believed.

They say goodbye as if they're waving off a ship from the harbour. I walk backwards through the gate, out of the hospital, with Roulin as my guide. Doctor Janson smiles, Director Bochet nods, and Doctor Rey, not only the youngest but also the shortest, says: 'Bonne chance.' And Roulin bellows: 'Bonne chance à vous!' Like that, cheerfully, we step out into the street.

'Wait,' says Roulin, 'the bag, you forgot your bag.' He turns around.

The street, which leads to the square in a gentle curve, is empty. It's cold. My breath forms a mist that's quickly erased, as if it isn't allowed to live here. Should I stay here standing at the door? I take a few steps further on my own.

There's no one to be seen in the square. The tolling of the church bell slowly sounds, and each beat remains hanging in the early, gentle light between the St Trophîme, the Hôtel de Ville and the obelisk. There I see an ice-cold sun-ray from a street in the east fall diagonally on the cobbles. This is what the city looks like when no one is watching – when there's no one there.

Then footsteps and an echo. Roulin approaches, silent now. When he gets close to me, he looks to one side and nods at the bag on his shoulder. Then he waits. When we cross the square I first take a deep breath. The air is so pale, so calm, almost comforting.

Doves. Crows.

I have forgotten everything.

Roulin nudges my shoulder. 'I'd like to tell you that I have all the time in the world, but unfortunately it isn't so.' And he starts talking about all his obligations, all the obligations of a patriarch, which he has to fulfil before he has to say goodbye to his family tomorrow and step onto the train for Marseilles. We walk across the paving stones and other people gradually come into view. Men and women. They all greet Roulin, Roulin tips his cap or bellows a name, depending on the history he has with these citizens. They look at me. A pair of delicate little ladies turn their upper bodies to look at me as I pass and suddenly I feel like waving my arms wide and screeching and biting them to death.

'We have to stop at Jeanne's first,' Roulin says. 'I gave her the job of tidying up your house, and knowing her she must have finished. She has the keys.'

Tidying up. That doesn't seem like the most important thing to me, Roulin, it wasn't so dirty. But okay. I feel like speaking out. I also don't feel like walking any further. The air isn't fresh any more.

'Thwack! Cut your whole head off! Go to hell! Cut your whole head off!'

Children.

'Go home!' Roulin shouts.

We enter the neighbourhood where I was looking for the Italians with Benoît and Michel. So this is where Jeanne lives. This street, the next street, that house. Roulin knocks. I have to grab hold of the doorpost because my legs suddenly start shaking from tiredness. We hear some life inside, some movement, and then the door opens. It's Jeanne; she looks at us. Roulin begins speaking: 'I told you I'd come and pick up the keys, so that's what I've come to do...' But in the meantime Jeanne has already looked at me and turned her scared little face away to go into the room and get the keys.

She's always kept herself invisible from me. She cleans when I'm not there, when I leave she slips in through the door, and I don't believe that she secretly feels like the lady of the house, as housemaids do. She leaves no traces behind.

The door is made out of planks, hammered together. The doorpost I'm leaning on sags down under my weight and I'm already imagining it snapping and myself falling into the broken bits. Jeanne comes shuffling back, drops the key into Roulin's outstretched hand, and shuts the door. On your feet. I'm going home. To work. Things are tidied up. That's how it goes.

There are people standing in the street, in a little group. In this neighbourhood the visitors are always closely watched. They're not saying anything, I think because Roulin is here. Roulin is a friend. 'We're going, we're going!' he says and holds the key high up in front of him like a star.

Walk for a little while and get warmer, then everything will feel less heavy. I've gone for walks day after day, I have enough strength in me. I think of Doctor Rey, who looked after me. His face always has a doctor's graveness, even though he is inexperienced. Masculine, but not like Milliet, more pensive, contemplative. That will keep him away from all the other things in life.

I don't remember anything out of all the things Rey told me last week in the hospital. Only the aggression, the remains of that I still feel in my body. Rah! Rah!

We arrive by the shrubs, next to my square. I'm suddenly afraid of what I might encounter, soon, when we cross the square and walk down to the house like the people did to look through the windows at the two painters painting Marie.

Shadows. Thwack! Thwack! Rah! Off with your head!

There it is. We avoid the puddles on the sandy square. Roulin goes to the door with the key, but wants to look in through the window first. Jeanne must have thoroughly got down to the business of cleaning. Everything to the side, or maybe everything outside, and then scrub. Maybe the furniture is still outside or someone has taken it away and I'll have to argue to get back what is mine. But the studio

71

looks familiar. Dusty, even. Nothing is lost yet.

'God damn it,' Roulin says. He looks like he wants to kick the door in. He's holding a piece of paper in his fist, a letter, which he's pulled from the door. 'Closed off by the police,' he says. 'That's not what we agreed. Come with me, I'm going to sort this out for you. They'll listen to me, they've always done that and, God damn it, that's what they'll do now.'

This anger was just a performance. He's in his element now, leading me to the police station. His beard has recently acquired a certain gleam, just like his shiny buttons and his eyes and his forehead. Still, I'm happy that he will handle this for me. 'I'll stay here,' I say.

'Just wait here, I'll put everything in order, all will be signed, sealed and delivered.'

I look inside again. 'The Three Graces', 'The Grape Harvest', the nude back of the farmer woman in the hay – Gauguin's canvases are still there in the studio. Is he coming back? It's the type of thought you keep at a distance because it's not worth anything on closer inspection. A small piece of tin. Gauguin used to do the housekeeping. He cooked on the stove, and counted the money, and said which groceries we needed to get. And in the meantime he painted. That's how you should live. He spoke to Jeanne while they both did their work around the house. Maybe more. I was always away, outside, I was only here to roll into bed exhaustedly, or to beg for help, for money, for company.

It would have been better if I had gone with Roulin after all. Now, I'm standing here waiting by what is no longer my house, it's more Roulin's house than mine, or Jeanne's, or the gendarme's whose arse Roulin is currently kissing, the gendarme with his moustache and his suit. I imagine them like this in the gendarmerie: 'I'll walk with you to open the door in a bit, but wait a minute, wait a minute,' and then he first shows off all the new things that they've received: leather gaiters, pretty flannel uniform jackets and – 'handsome weapons' – the slender carbines spread out on a table in an another room.

But Roulin comes back quickly, shaking his head. 'No problem! I've solved it, it was a misunderstanding.' But we still can't go inside because we have to wait for one of the gendarmes to come and open the door for us. 'Then we'll go next door,' Roulin says, 'to have a drink, I have deserved it, I would say. And you too, of course.' We go into the café. We have a cognac and an absinthe. Nothing's changed here. There are some men sitting at the side, a small one and a big, strong one, who look like they're brothers. Jakob and Ezau. I recognise their faces; hopefully they don't recognise me.

They do. They're not going to ignore me. There they are.

'Roulin! My man! How is it in Marseilles?'

'Not bad, gentlemen, not bad.'

They've come to sit with us now and are looking sneeringly in my direction.

I quickly take another absinthe. Another one. We're all drinking. They're waiting for someone to break the silence and set them at ease. Roulin does that. 'And Vincent,' he says, 'is also feeling well again.'

'I'm a painter and we have these quirks,' I say.

I quickly offer them something to drink, which they naturally accept.

'And now? Are you better now?' Ezau says. His eyes circle around the bandage on my head. It's too tight, I feel my veins throbbing; I'd forgotten about it but now I can feel the stiffened fabric. I must look like a housemaid and that would explain their chuckling. All three of them are sitting there chuckling. We drink one glass after another. The café fills up in no time, I don't know what everyone's come for, but they're standing around us. I try to look out of the window through the gaps between all the people.

The bare trees on the pavements, standing in a line. If you look at the branches, they jolt further and further up. Thwack! A little black dog trots around the corner. Looking here, looking there. Its owner is also there, in a black suit, looking at nothing and walking straight ahead.

The pain in my neck keeps growing stronger, as if the circle of the wound is continuously widening and the cut deepening. Someone tries to push the bandage aside, either Jakob or Ezau, to show the others what's underneath it. I've drunk so much that I'm letting them do it, it's the easiest way. I look at Roulin, who has closed his eyes.

Later I have to lean on Roulin's massive body to come out of the café, into the street. I keep slipping from his shoulder, but his arm around my waist helps keep me on my feet. He's pushed his hand into my side, I can feel my guts. We arrive at the house. The door is open. And the gap in that doorway will suck me inside as soon as Roulin lets go of me.

I screw all the caps on the tubes. That's what I'll do from now on. Caps on all the tubes, even if it might not be the right cap on the right colour. The work is good, today I worked on a sky and it's become more powerful. The work is good. Without noticing, I have just spent another five minutes looking at it. I wipe my hands clean, tomorrow I'll continue. Someone knocks on the window and then on the door. Through the window I see a man take up his position, waiting until I open up. It's the pedantic gendarme, this friend of Roulin's. I don't know his name but I know him and he knows me. I open the door, he follows me inside. He looks smart. Boots, belt, gloves. Cap in his hand.

He lets his eyes roam through the studio. I've only seen him from a distance before, and then those eyes always seemed drowsy, like the eyes of a man who likes a good sleep and a good drink, but that's not true: his eyes are drooping from tiredness, but also attentive. It's now too late for it, actually, but we shake hands. Gryenque, that's his name. He is taller than me.

He says that he must be disturbing me in my work. I nod. He has a letter in his hand. A document. Trouble.

I start to talk a bit about how I'm working on the varnishes, that some of the canvases are already dry, that I roll them up to send to Paris. The light is on in the studio, because it's getting darker outside. Clouds of intense dark blue. There's going to be a storm before midday.

'Paris,' says Gryenque, 'and what happens with them then, in Paris?'

'They're exhibited there. My brother is an art dealer.'

'I don't believe I know what such a painting might cost.' He gestures with his right hand to no specific canvas. His voice is deep and resonating. Accentless. In different clothes, with a slightly straighter back and a stare that is more direct, he could be a diplomat.

'Some are 400, some 100 francs,' I say. I continue talking about the prices on the art market for a while, but I can see that there's absolutely no point. Gryenque is ignoring what I'm saying. Until now he's been friendly, maybe out of shyness and also out of sympathy, but he's come to carry out a task and, actually, should have established his authority immediately. In the meantime it's started to rain, hard gusts of wind and water on the square and against the house. Gryenque walks to the door and now lets in two wet gendarmes who were standing there waiting. They are young fellows, who stay standing by the door because they're not sure what's expected of them, and shyly nod at me. They know me, they're drinking mates in the café, but they don't repeat Gryenque's mistake and silently look past me.

Then they jump, because a dog has slipped in alongside them. A small brown dog that for a second looks around at all the men in the room, and then starts moving and sniffing along the walls, suddenly and quickly, as if it's repeatedly walking through legs.

The two young policemen look to me for a sign that this is in order, that the dog is supposed to be here, and I stick out my hand towards the wet animal, which it briefly smells. Suppose I am looking after this dog.

Gryenque takes the floor. 'We,' he nods his head towards his companions who are waiting, 'we've come to take you with us to the hospital.'

That's what I'd thought and it's turned out to be true.

'Take me with you?' I say. You have to say it all out loud now, Gryenque, go on and read out the letter. But he says nothing. He holds up the document.

'Why?'

He looks through the window. The small square. The first shower has blown over, but a new one is arriving. A bit of sunshine has managed to stream in through the layer of clouds.

'The people don't feel safe.'

I go back to work.

'You've assaulted women. Harassed children. It's all written down.'

76

'Assaulted,' I say.

'Mme Feuiller. You've held Mme Feuiller hostage and groped her. You said obscene things.'

Liliane Feuiller. Held hostage and groped? Yes, danced with, you mean. I danced with her and lifted her up in the air. I also talked to her, I remember. About a bit of everything, I told her about my life, she looked at me laughingly, about painting, and maybe also about sex, certainly, we just talked about it, I made no indecent proposals. And we just danced.

I look at Gryenque. It's impossible to explain it to him, it would be meaningless. He thinks that I'm crazy. He's looking for signs. Maybe I should scare him off.

Suddenly our attention is grabbed by the dog, scratching the floor with its nails. It's become foolhardy and is running around through the studio and now barking too. I hear it piss in the corner behind the table and when it goes on running it sprays its piss everywhere, its hind paws as wide as can be. Against the paintings, too. I shout 'Hey, hey!' The other fellows are also getting involved now. I open the door in the hope that the dog will take the hint, but it carries on running round in circles looking unhappy. The fellows try to drive it to the door, but the dog looks frenzied. It suddenly stops in the middle of the room, braces itself on its back paws and, yelping, starts pooping. One of the fellows boots it in the side and the other on its back and they keep kicking the dog like that, metre by metre, towards the door. They hesitate for a second when they realise that the dog is clearly trying to escape but at the same time frenetically trying to empty its bowels; a doubtful dog between a rock and a hard place, that's a difficult thing to see. But dogs don't doubt things, and a dog is not a human being, and they kick it hard one more time and then it only needs only one sweep of an arm and the dog runs, whining in fear, out of the door.

Benoît and Michel. Those are not their names, of course, but I call them that.

I go and sit on the chair. They must see how calm I am. It is clear that I need a moment to process what is happening, right? To let it get through to me that I will be locked up. Gryenque now opens an envelope that he still had in his hand and gives me a sheet of paper. He sighs while doing it.

Oh... oh...

It is a list of names.

'Dutch citizen Vincent has demonstrated that he is not in possession of his full mental abilities. We live in FEAR, for our wives and our children. In the name of safety he must, as soon as possible, be taken away, to his family, an institution for the mentally ill or another place OUTSIDE ARLES.'

Lefrevre, Roulin, everyone.

I know why this is happening, I understand it. That's how it goes. *Why don't you act like it then?*

'You just have to get your things. Just be calm. We'll wait for a little bit. Just get your things.'

I can't expect much more from him. He's also seen me drunk sometimes, and angry, and he's read what it says on this piece of paper. And are they not right? I lift women up into the air. I sometimes shout. Here, the people on that list, they've seen all of that, most I don't know by name but I do know their faces just like they know my face, and they're right. Roulin is on the list too. If Roulin says it, then it is so.

Gryenque has stood up again. 'We could also come and pick up some things later. I think we have to go now.' Is he in a hurry because I've been sitting looking at him for so long? Do I now also have the look of a madman?

'My apologies,' I say. 'I am making you wait a long time, indeed. But you've caught me off guard, you understand?'

Gryenques nods, but says: 'Surely you won't have been that surprised.'

'No, maybe not.'

Of course, now I'm looking at him for far too long again. 'Listen,' I want to say. 'Listen…' But what should he listen to? Gryenques, the diplomat. He looks a bit apologetic, he understands that it's painful. He can sympathise somewhat. Let me tell him something about myself. Touch a tender spot. Establish contact. With his thoughtful expression – and there I was thinking that he was a spitfire – he will tell his wife about me this evening. 'No luck, that man has got no luck. It could've gone like that with me too, in another life.' She strokes his neck. They've sat like this more often recently, his wife thinks, and she says: 'Darling, you do have luck, you have this life', and they feel happy and sad at the same time. But to have him talk like that with his wife I first have to tell him something and to tell him something I have to dig something up from the mush inside. But everything immediately flows away.

Something.

'I come from Paris,' I say. Paris. A flash of a street. The front window of a café. The smell of…

When you die. Then everything flows away just like that. The memories that you try to bring back and give form to. But they are so fleeting, your memories, your place among people, you've always seen it the wrong way, that's how it is your whole life. That's how you die.

Benoît now grabs my upper arm. He pulls, come along. I jerk my arm loose and ram my elbow into his chest.

The other one now does the same with me. His hand on my upper arm. Gryenque sighs again. That man actually sits by his wife on the bed, grieving. But not about me, God damn it. Then, they both grab me, pull my arms behind my back, my head backwards. I wrench, I wrench, I wrench. I tear my body apart. Swing my legs forward, Gryenque is standing there, merciless, and I kick him where I can reach. Then I bang backwards onto the floor, lie there, and they pull at my shoulders, someone kicks me in the side. It looks like my shoulders are elongated, they pull me across the floor of the studio by my shoulders and now I feel how rough this floor is, tubes, caps, knives, how the dust forms ridges, the piss of the dog, the doorstep, the sand of the square. I jerk. Ah, ah, rain, rain. People stop and stand in the rain. People, if you saw what I now see...

People, come. Come and join me. Listen. You're standing around me to listen to me.

Come. *Empty inside? Without memories?* Dozens, thousands of memories! Listen.

The first memory is the green garden in Zundert. It was my mother's birthday. We had guests. Uncle Cent, aunt Mien, extra chairs were shoved in, but I stood at the back of the garden, which was over-abundant and wild, full of plants that had grown metres tall in a few days. Himalayan balsams. Giant hogweed. I stood between the thick stalks and leaves and shiny seed pods that burst at the slightest touch. It was that warm. The air was mad from all the insects dashing round and round. And I was looking at the back of the vicarage. The windows with their dented glass were half open, held back by slats that would otherwise be lying on the windowsill. I couldn't see the people inside, sometimes a shadow or a reflection. Their voices formed no more than a thin stream, which had already been blown away by the wind by the time it reached me, through the window and along the flower beds full of unripe raspberries and currants. But I kept hearing my name being mentioned between the inaudible worries and reproaches. 'Vincent. Vincent, who...' The muffled voices saying 'Vincent'.

The second memory is a globule of spit on yellow skin. It was noisy, always noisy in and around the house in The Hague, people often walked close by the window, even at night. The baby was asleep. I sat in the chair in the dark. Unable to do anything the whole day. In the corner of the room stood a small bed with my wife on it. My wife, Sien. She was mean and nasty, but she couldn't help it. If you knew about her past... She was sick and lay on a bed without covers. She was sleeping, but maybe not. In the evenings there was no difference between being exhausted, or asleep, not looking at each other. I looked at her sick body. A corpse. And yet there were some men left who for a few cents... Above her chest lay a large drop of fluid. I looked after her, I felt compassion for her, and yet I didn't love her.

That's what I thought about as I looked at that poor, dirty body in all that noise.

The third memory is soup in the darkness. The darkness was the darkness that reigned over the mines where I tried to help so many sick, poor and miserable people. Everyone was black, the women had black stripes on their faces and hands and the men were poor, black devils. The sun remained hanging behind the grey clouds. One night there was a flash, a bolt of lightning, not in the sky but in the earth, and the workers in the mineshafts got scorched or suffocated in the dust and smoke. I looked after one such devil who had survived. He didn't have any skin left and was swathed in grey bandages. I unwrapped them from his sticky body and said 'Easy now' and washed him and smeared him in oil. Olive oil, it was. 'Easy, easy now.' One month, two months. I prayed for him, I spoke with his wife and prayed with her. Myself, I slept on a plank. I wanted to feel the cold and the hunger, because for Jesus too, anything was enough. But they came and brought me soup anyway, a few times. That, I couldn't stop. Foul soup it was, it made you want to spit it out. I just lay there and watched the dark sky through which nightingales flew, night birds, I mean bats.

The fourth memory is Theo. My brother. His cheeks sliced open and a knife in his gullet. The black handle was faded and greasy, like the grip of an old tool. It might have been of ebony, carved with silver. It was stuck in his throat and therefore no longer shined and looked like dry fish skin. My dear brother, who always plodded on and was sometimes too generous with his blessing.

The fifth memory is my father, who had just come home from the church service. He was a minister. After the service at the church, at which my mother and I and my brother and sisters were the first to arrive – we went and sat at the front and were the last to get up to leave – after returning home I was often called to his room. I had to go to his office, the room he also used on Sundays to rest and as the headquarters for all his activities. When he came home he would first walk to this room, to the left and front of the house, to hang up his jacket, look through the papers on the desk, straighten them out with his fingertips and, sometimes, to receive parishioners. That's where I had to wait for him. I don't remember any more what I had done wrong. Shouted, maybe. Been cheeky. Looked angry. *Made people sad.* Every Sunday I waited there for him to come home. 'Why did you act like that?' he kept asking. 'Why did you shout?' Questions to which no answer was possible. This time he asked nothing. He came in, closed the door, slowly wriggled himself out of his black jacket and smoothed his clothes. He seemed to be lost in his thoughts, closed up, but he wasn't. He drank a glass of milk, sitting down and looking outside. Then he walked up to me and held my head tightly with both his hands and looked inquisitively into my eyes. He pulled down one of my eyelids. He felt the glands in my neck. He enclosed my skull in his hands. My father was a man with a large head and small hands. He felt my skull as if he wanted to explore it. His hands were the cold hands of a doctor. I could tell by his eyes that he found himself confronted with something he couldn't handle. There had always existed a strain of helplessness in my father, but now it took on a sad and painful dimension.

The sixth memory is Rachel's hair. Artfully pinned up. She had twisted her hair into strands and pinned them up on her head like a diadem. She sat with her back to me in front of a dressing-table mirror. A kimono of cream-coloured silk was thrown around her shoulders. Her arms moved and the sleeves slid down along her smooth skin. The stillness of the room. The gleaming hair. Her busy arms.

I said, 'You have to go back downstairs, of course.'

But she said: 'I feel like staying here.' You have to know that we'd just fucked, I'll just say it. A crude pleasure, and maybe vulgar, but it was what I had always wanted. I remember the deep satisfaction it gave me, the awareness that she was obliging to me. Rachel was a sweet girl, you should know. But the sensation itself, skin against skin, the feeling of her deep vagina or the palm of her hand on my body, everything else that I must have felt that I can't bring to mind now. Before I couldn't imagine it and then later it was gone. Longing. I sat behind her and touched her hair with my hand. The solidly pinned-up hair, that's what it feels like. But skin... Feelings from the heart, only those.

The seventh memory is a dog in a field. A brown dog, which in the evening light looked reddish. It was fit, a hunting dog, I think. It had appeared next to me during one of my walking tours in Belgium. I had left before sunrise that morning and now the twilight was setting in again, after a rough day: a lot of sun and a lot of wind. My knees felt like solid cement. I was so hungry. Then, suddenly, this dog was walking next to me, through a rolling field. I walked along the path, the dog next to it, through the wheat overgrown with bindweed and withered cornflowers. It walked with me for kilometres. Now and then it would stray, or stop to look into the distance, but then it would spring back into motion again. Suddenly it swerved to the right and just continued walking, away from me; for a long time I could watch it walking through the rolling landscape, with tears in my eyes, of course.

You see, one memory after another. Thousands, millions.

***

People, come. Listen. The whole square is filled, you've kept room free for me. What does it mean to have regrets? And how is one supposed to act upon them? That's what I'll talk about.

Someone has regrets when they realise that everything went differently from how they thought it would. A boy who eats at the table with his parents, goes to school,

84

argues and laughs. And every time his parents reprimand him and look him in the eyes, they feel a heavy sensation because *something is wrong with him*. And despite all the signs and warnings, all the conflicts and crises, it takes almost his entire life before he realises it. My father saw it a long time ago. My mother, my brother, Gauguin saw it. My father saw the symptoms even when I was a child, he felt them on my skull with his hands. And the sky, heaven, has all my life enclosed my skull like the hands of my father. Gauguin too. I thought that we just had arguments, differences of opinion between outspoken people, daggers drawn, maybe. But that wasn't it: they were dealing with a sick person. They wanted to send me to an institution, even then. And I jumped on a boat and on a train! I go here, I go there, I work and I work, Paris, the South, to start up a studio! Everywhere it's obvious, everywhere they spot it immediately.

You, all the people of Arles, saw it immediately.

And how is one intended to act in that case?

You lay down your clothes and go out into the cold. You take off your clothes, that's what I mean. Naked. Save the food from your mouth. Avoid company. You have to pray. You have to be pure. You don't need anything. Be a better son, a better friend. Try not to be a painter, but to help your fellow human beings. Sleep little, drink a bit of water, eat a crust of bread and work. Then you die.

I try to think of dying with a smile and without the emptiness of the mown field – which was yesterday still tall and lush in the trembling August light and is now flat and bristly – and I imagine the farmer who does his hard work in peace and later is no longer a mower, but a sower. Why, then, do I resist death so? Why do I scream so much?

***

People on the square, come, listen. The eighth memory is a 500-franc note. At the Gare de Lyon. The note between the

85

fingers of Theo's white, slender hand, right before it disappears into my fist. All that time in Paris when we lived together, it was getting harder and harder for me to stand his presence. His unreasonableness – his lack of vision and daring – the cash book in which he kept count of all my spending, down to a centime, so that I had to feel guilty if I so much as went to the barber – his categorical refusal to give in to my arguments – I still remember how he sat at his table working and then said 'I don't hear you, Vincent, I don't hear you, I'm just carrying on', as if he was humming a song – how he was constantly breathing down my neck and one time started crying because I'd used an old pair of trousers to clean my brushes – everything, everything was a reproach. But when we were standing at the station, we'd lived through a few calm, peaceful days. Happy days. I'd made myself useful around the house by tidying up, by helping Theo out where I could. He was struggling with problems in his work that I couldn't quite comprehend but that he wanted to talk about a lot. I let him talk, without giving my opinion. We listened to music on his gramophone to calm his nerves. At the station he must have thought: my brother must really hate me, to abandon me like this now.

The ninth memory is a painting. It's a painting that I made myself, but I can't name the specific work now, I've made so many, it was a painting that I was working on at the time. I remember the day in Nuenen when I painted the ramshackle tower by the churchyard. My arms were moving. Looking at the sky and at the landscape, or at the farmers and the fields, the weavers and their looms, the hay, the corn, the vineyards in the autumn sun. I was being carried along, my eyes looked, my arms moved. One discovery after another. No one had seen it before. My confidence was inconceivably great and my happiness was inconceivably great.

The tenth memory is the dance with a woman on Bastille Day. Everyone was dancing, the whole town, the small orchestra played music that everyone loved and the lanterns were bobbing back and forth. We threw our arms into the air – me and the woman, a chubby woman with freckles, but then I suddenly saw terror in her eyes, as if I was a satyr. I looked down: I saw my legs. But in her eyes they were goat's legs and my laughter in her ears was the sneer of the devil. I still danced on, but it seemed as if everyone was listening to my hooves pounding on the floor, up and down, and the party continued only after I'd left.

The eleventh memory is the smack of an open hand on my head. The hand belonged to Agostina Segatori. You know her. She once sat on my lap to cut my hair and also once stuck her hand down my trousers and whispered 'Vincent'. And: 'You belong here, here with us.' She gave me that smack in the presence of all the Italians and the other people that sat eating and drinking in the café. She hit me awkwardly on the top of the head, and then spat. And I longed for her so much at that time that I interpreted it as something sexual, I was drooling, and only after a while did I understand and left her café with my tail between my legs, and never went back there again.

The twelfth memory is of the sky above this square, the Place Lamartine in Arles. I was stretched out by my shoulders and hauled through the sand and the stones, looking up. I thought: the richness of those skies, the sea-like grey, with thin blue veins, the pink, the absorbed purple, if you could only see this. But I realised that it was now all about what I couldn't see. The people who remained standing in the square, the windows of the cafés, the men that came to light up the lamps, the rhythm of the city and her inhabitants and the gendarmes that pulled me out of that city like a splinter.

The last memory is the garden in Zundert. I stood at the back of the garden, the plants were growing around me, and I heard people in the house talking to each other.

MARCH 1889

To move my body, lift my arms up from the sheets, bend my legs, move my head to and fro – I have to dredge up the strength for this from sources that have long been cut off.

Through my veins slides sand. My eyes are closed. I am awake, I have woken up. The sunlight through the window is so bright. I can't open my eyes. What would happen if I did anyway? When my eyelids open, the sunlight will destroy my nerves.

The curtains are still open. It's so dark here in the evenings that they don't have to be shut, last night there were even no stars to be seen.

Maybe I've already been awake for a long time.

That's why I'm here, because I can't move. He was so right to send me here. So justified. Good of my brother. He did what my father would have wanted to do. In a hospital I would have to let myself be taken care of, at home I would have to fight the people off, and in an institution like this I can stay motionless.

Turned to stone.

Footsteps sound in the hallway. It's time to have breakfast. They pound on the door. 'Monsieur Vincent?' they say. 'Wake up. Breakfast is ready.'

Let me sink away into the sand.

A pain now develops in my arm. A burning spot.

I've had it all this time. The pain only now breaks into my consciousness, but it already feels familiar. An intense pain in my upper arm. It comes from an animal and the animal hisses and keeps putting its spider legs on my arm. On my chest. My face. I am naked.

A bee.

I've now straightened myself up and am sitting almost on the edge of the bed. When I sit on the edge of the bed I have to support my head with two hands.

I turn my head and look at my arm, at the bee-stings. I think that it stung twice. There's nothing to see.

I let my head hang between my knees.

I can't turn to stone like this, God damn it.

'Monsieur Vincent? Breakfast.'

They don't shut up. They keep going on until I make my way towards the breakfast hall. Let me sink away. My arm now feels as if it's been crushed between two rocks, but, almost unbelievably, I seem to be able to move it. A single bee that can cause so much pain to a human body. Water, to cool it down. If I stand up, I immediately stumble. I fall through the air, without a single grasp. I roll on the floor. So fast. Here I lie. I feel a mark on my forehead where I hit the table, but no pain. None whatsoever. The jug is still standing, I notice; it's made of glass, of course it could have broken and spat out shards, but apparently it was a case of balance. From this perspective the room looks torn apart, but I can find my bearings. I straighten up, but of course I would prefer to stay lying down. It was wonderful to be lying down. But I'm moving. Up.

Monsieur Vincent opens the door and enters the corridor. The murmur of my fellow patients can be heard here. The poor wretches. They walk around like someone's holding them up by the skin of their necks. Sometimes they're so crazy that they scream and foam at the mouth, and sometimes they're so crazy that they seem completely normal, just misplaced and therefore so penetrating, like people who accost you in your dreams. They lay a hand on your shoulder and talk to you, like him, I don't know his name, a man as old as me who's always clutching the same spoon in his hand and wants to whisper in my ear so that I feel his revolting spittle. 'No,' I say, 'no!' I open a door and step to the side, out of the corridor. I stagger for a second, because I've put my foot on a step. Outside.

The air is surprisingly cold and rapidly spreads itself through my chest. I'm allowed to go into the garden, but now I'm here and there's nothing to see.

Let me sink away.

Further down the attendant is doing something. The attendant, I always call him that in my mind. His name is Franck. He bends down, comes back up. Moves something. There's a barrow next to him. He's probably already noticed me. He knows exactly what I'm allowed and what I'm not allowed to do. Soon he'll have to come with me, outside the fence. He must dislike painters. I walk outside his line of vision.

The wall, that goes around the whole institution. A fence at the front. I can just about see over it. There the fields, here the garden.

Outside this fence, into those fields. Why? I've asked for it myself, but I think I shouldn't do it yet. In the very early sunshine like now it's a surface with dark shapes of hills in the background and maybe trees. But what will become visible later? Luckily the fence hasn't swung open yet.

Beautiful is not the word for this garden. The attendant maintains it, and now and then gets 'help' from patients like me. Here and there it resembles a real garden. Flowerbeds. Roses, irises, marigolds, oleanders that spread like wildfire. The irises are blue and white and stand together in a bunch. The stalks and the long leaves are emerald green with soft yellow hearts. The leaves wriggle up like evening gowns, it is a green crowd. The ground between the plants is brown and yellow and pink. The flowers of the white irises look so much more delicate, almost ghostly, among the blue ones, the blue ones are of thick daubs of colour, from soft and sea blue to cobalt and even Prussian blue. You have to put them together, all these blue irises, with the orange marigolds in the background as a contrast. We used to have these irises too. And also marigolds, by the way. I stand in the garden from the past as a child, which is the memory that always plays, even if it doesn't have to mean anything. *There is something going on in the house or on the street, and I'm standing in this garden, waiting.*

The lush blue irises that have overgrown the canvas, diagonally, the soil in the foreground, the marigolds behind it even more fiery than they are, and one or two white ones, left or right. They are so different.

And the grass around it. The grass is mown. That way it looks even simpler, even more beautiful. To make a painting from simple grass. Of course that's what Franck is doing, mowing the grass. He's put his scythe against the barrow, he rakes the clippings together in between the flowerbeds and bushes and scoops them up between his spread-out arms and throws them sideways onto the barrow, where they sink in like a cushion. Maybe it's for the rabbits or the chickens. I will ask him later what he's going to do with them. His face is brown and copper-coloured, like everyone else's here. He doesn't sweat easily, but his serious face is shiny and his mouth is open and when the grass is all lying in the barrow, he quickly walks away from the sunlight to a space under one of the pine trees. He works with the sluggish movement of cattle. His brown, thick hair is combed. How old is he? Almost forty, I think, older than me, but stronger and not sick.

'Bonjour,' I say.

'Bonjour.'

'Il fait beau.'

'Oui.'

'Can I help?'

'All right.'

Only a few weeks ago I kicked him in the back. He doesn't look at me, a look of understanding is not in his character. He bends down and works.

'You don't have to worry,' I say, 'no more kicking.' It was a kick that must have hurt for a few days. Under his ribs, in the soft part. He got in my way, then. And I thought that he had sent the police after me.

'No,' Franck says, 'it's going better now, right?'

'Yes.'

'Yes, you were ill. Eating paint. Drinking turpentine.'

'Yes.'

'That's behind you now.'

He picks up the scythe and starts cutting again, with confident strokes. I stay under the pine tree gathering the grass. It has grown tall, the blades are as long as my arms. Fragrant weeds in between. They move over one another, the cut blades and stalks, if I sweep my fingers through them.

'Soon we're going outside the fence, on our way, mister, I've heard.' He talks more loudly, now that he's standing further down. 'Are you going to paint?'

'Yes,' I say.

I help him now until he's finished and tomorrow or the day after he will help me.

November 1889

Franck walks behind me on the path and not beside me, I don't know why. Because he has to look after me, because he's my attendant. Or because he'd rather be somewhere else. We go into a gorge, a small gorge with loose stones, shrubs and sometimes spicy green and purple colours. Shrubs. Toss them with your hand and you'll smell the sharp wood and the life in the leaves.

We hardly talk. We accept each other that way.

We stop. I set up the easel and immediately start painting. Franck goes to sit down on a stone like on a stool, holding it in balance with his weight. As determinedly as he walks, like a ploughing horse, so he sits too. Waiting. He has an earthenware pipe that, on these walks, he puts into his mouth when he sits down and afterwards doesn't move any more. He looks out over the land and makes plans for his own work. He looks at the sky, the weather, that way he knows if he'll have to mow again tomorrow.

Painting. I paint like a madman, I know that. But that's how I stir up the fire in me, how I keep it going, that goes automatically. The ravine is beautiful, it is passable and inhospitable at the same time, the face of the rock towers up high and the stones have slowly rolled or shifted from their places through the course of centuries. A painting like this, when I imagine how others would look at it, when I imagine what Theo or Gauguin would think of it, then my confidence is intact. If I show this in Arles, they will find it beautiful.

I now see myself lugging this painting around the city.

I stop by to see Marie, who has grown so ill. Roulin told me in his letter, which he had composed like a newspaper full of pompously formulated notices from Arles, about her 'women's illness, always so sad and weak'. She will like the paintings I've made of her recently. They are in the style of Mr Gauguin, 'Mr Gauguin!', I based them on his drawing because she admired it so much and understood it, but there's more to it than that, I wanted to bring a certain comfort to it.

If I want to go to Arles, I have to submit a request. Franck will have to come with me. A day trip out, and then safely back to my room. I try to consider such a request through his eyes. *What kind of sense does it make? Does he want to have some fun? An excursion? To shake people's hands? And when he's walking through the streets of Arles, is he walking through a street or through a memory? 'Look, there's the café where I often used to eat. Look, my house, it's still there. Look, here, mister and missus, how are you? Give your children my regards!' An idiot.*

Marie won't understand it either. She'll hear me out and be happy when I leave.

Yes.

But I also feel a different kind of illness in me. My cells are bubbling, during the walk here I had to stop a few times to calm down. The urge to turn over stones, to see what happens, to go into motion and to seize situations. Be among people. And at the same time I'm shitting in my pants from dread. The looks, the rejection, the invisibility, everything has changed and I don't understand anything any more, someone comes around the corner and starts shouting at me without me understanding why.

But I feel like shitting in my pants where I stand.

I'm not going to say that to Franck, though. I say: 'Do you feel like a little trip to the city?'

Franck says nothing, but frowns for a moment. Unfathomable, such a frown. He examines how I paint. What does he think of it? He thinks it's nothing. Something a crazy person makes. Those irises, he found them beautiful. Plants. The colours he liked, he said, and looked happily surprised.

Maybe I should go back to Paris. Theo will find space for me in his house, I'll paint, I'll sleep, I won't be any trouble.

No, that can't happen. Maybe never again.

And to Arles?

I paint a man in a ravine. 'Look,' I say, 'that's you, Franck.' He walks up to me and bends down over the canvas. He's short-sighted. Then he looks at me, again with such a frown. But he laughs as well, just like Milliet would do. His hair is very short, almost as short as my beard. There's a lot of grey among the brown that you see only from close up. With his thin face full of freckles and his light brown eyes he doesn't seem to take life so seriously, but he does, he just accepts everything as it is. 'I hope,' he says, 'that I'm not as ugly as that painting.'

Franck is my guide. Because he is with me, I can move through the landscape. Would I dare to without him? Theo was my guide in Paris. Milliet was my guide in Arles, when he walked beside me nothing could happen to me. Gauguin too. No, not Gauguin.

Imagine if Theo was standing next to me. He would look at the canvas for a moment, he'd say one word about it and then keep looking. With his thoughts elsewhere.

But to Arles.

I can see the people in front of me, two by two, or in small groups, in large companies, walking through the streets and through the parks. The light of the cafés. I want to go back one time. Everything is different now. I don't live there any more, I am a guest. The good in all these people... We drink a glass, I tell them about life in a madhouse, Roulin talks about life in Marseilles, we discuss the work on the land, 'Are there a lot of seasonal workers?', 'Do you remember those Italians, Vincent, we scared them good for a moment, but caused no pain.'

Don't think about it.

Franck wants to go. I'm suddenly aware of him again, he just sits there waiting, dead quiet, and that too makes him look like a horse. I don't say that to him, there are so many good characteristics he shares with horses, a bigger

97

compliment is perhaps unthinkable, but he would take it the wrong way. He treats me like a patient, they all do here. *Bring him here, bring him there, let him paint, give him a pat on the shoulder.* The way he always walks behind me, it irritates me so much and now I know why: we form a procession, me in front, him behind with all the things, a procession in which I'm the dead dog.

I turn around and Franck isn't there. Is he not sitting behind this rock? No, he's disappeared. Maybe he's climbed further up to be able to pee or poo out of sight. I just keep working, but listen for all possible sounds. The wind, regular gusts of wind. I could paint in the same slow rhythm.

He still isn't back after fifteen minutes. 'Franck!' I call out, and as that blows through the air, I feel a sensation of freedom. To run through there, against the wind, and if I have moved out of the gorge before Franck is back, he would never find me again. Gone. But I could always do that, walk away. He wouldn't have kept me.

He was sitting there diagonally behind me, he didn't walk past me. Then he must have gone up there. Can I leave the easel here like this? No, it'll soon get blown over. I take the canvas off it and place it against a rock, in the lee. I put the paint in the box, tidy everything up, that means it's done for today. Where should I leave it? Imagine if someone comes along, unattended things on the path.

Where could he be? Maybe Franck is the one who chose freedom. Huh, no, he's not like that, but on the other hand: I see him as a horse, and horses sooner or later go into a stampede.

I walk up. He must have gone this way. And immediately I see him, half lying down against the rock-face, and he raises his eyes towards me, which mitigates my fearful suspicions.

'What is it?' I say.

He waits until I've come closer. 'I fell.' He points towards his left knee. He holds his left leg stretched out. It is serious, no way around it.

'Do you want a drink?' I say.

He nods.

I think that the knee is broken. I feel sick looking at it, if he lifts up his leg, his knee will dangle. He doesn't want to talk about it. When I ask about what exactly happened, he does some pointing, 'stumbled there', but it seems as if he'd rather be left alone. People like him have been through this more often, they know exactly how to act and don't want to explain it to nitwits.

'I'll just fetch my things,' I say, 'and then I'll get help. Then they'll come to get you.'

'Good,' he says.

When I come back, he says: 'I can walk myself. You just go.'

'Stand up then.'

'In a bit.'

'Just stand up, if I see it works then I'll go.'

He looks straight ahead for a while, to gather his strength. Please let it work. Hold in your breath and then up with a jump, on the left leg. You see? Then I can go.

But no, that will never work.

Then I'll have to take him home, neither of us can accept that. He doesn't trust me to do that, and if he did trust me I would not be able to fulfil it. My God, I'll go, and make sure someone comes to get him. Why didn't you stay with him?

Franck has now stuck his leg under him like a spring. A moment later he braces himself with his hands in the sand and gravel and tenses his leg, even I feel how the muscles contort to their burning limit, but he can't go through with it.

'My God,' he says.

Paint on, work on, eat, that's what I want. But suddenly something in me shifts.

'I'll help you. We're going to see if we can try to get home.' I squat next to him, on his right side. Now he will have to put his arm around me, but it seems like he doesn't

99

understand that. His face is pale, covered in fermenting drops. Shouldn't we examine the knee? No, I'm way too scared of it. I now hold Franck tightly with my left arm, my hand in his armpit, and try to stand up. He doesn't give way. Before I know it, I'm standing next to him with my legs spread out, but my back is bent. I quickly let go and when I stand up straight and stretch my back I feel how stiff I am. The suppleness is completely gone from my body; when was it last there? I can't remember the last time.

The second time Franck cooperates. We get up at the same time, the first part is no problem, but after that we must take care not to be thrown off balance. He is leaning against me with his entire weight and I can provide counter-force. We stand. We both groan, I from exertion, he in pain.

I have given Franck a branch to use as a walking stick, I tied the easel and box and canvas onto my back, and with my left arm I'm supporting Franck. He walks slowly. I adjust my tempo, first by taking smaller steps, by stepping in the same rhythm as him, so slowly that the load on my back makes me wobble. Sometimes he stops. Then he stands there gasping for a moment, trying to let the pain fade away. At first, his right hand lies on my shoulder like a saddle bag, but his grip is becoming tighter and tighter and my arm is starting to feel numb. I try to distract him from the pain by talking and telling him stories and he spurs me on, as best he can, by repeatedly stammering 'yes'.

'Yes.'

He does walk along, Franck. As long as there's someone to walk along with, as long as I keep going and distract him a little bit, he won't stop. What should I tell him about? Trivialities. There's a curve, we're walking well, the sun is going down. When I stop talking, a soft moan comes through his lips in little waves. His fiery breath doesn't smell of food but of damp air. His torso is leaning against me and with every step he brushes his hip alongside mine. The muscle under his armpit is lying in my hand, I feel how the skin lies somewhat loosely on the flesh, just like mine, the body of men like us. In the meantime I go on talking.

'Yes.'

I tell him about the Netherlands, about the north that he's never seen. In the winter the geese migrate in lines across the sky. Peat fields. The sharp wind which dams up the water in the fens. It can be cold here too, but not so cold that the ground freezes. When you dig into the cold ground, the hollow chill rises up into your hands. The monotonous singing in the churches. Also hollow and cold, those churches. Grain, wheat, corn in the field. You see fields with grain a lot more often in the Netherlands than here. Long grain, or short, stiff heather. 'Those geese, I started talking about them because you always see them flying in twilight, like now, when it starts getting colder,' I say. 'Then they fly to the water to stay the night. The night falls, the whole of the Netherlands turns into a shadow, but then you hear those geese honking and you see those fleshy lumps flying overhead, so low that you could touch them. That's one of the beautiful things.'

'Yes.'

'This is the most terrible walk we've ever been on,' I say. It seems as if we have been out together already so many times, but if I think about it, the times can be counted on the fingers of two hands. Into the vineyards, the olive garden, a bit towards the hills, but always close to St Remy. They're my outings, of course, Franck comes along only because he has to, but he enjoys walking, and he also likes the quietness to just hang around a place without working. He always sees animals. He can let his thoughts wander to things.

He is not even scared of me.

'A friend of mine is sick,' I say. 'In Arles.'

Franck can talk, but only on the breath he takes as he puts his right leg forward, leaning on me and the cane.

'A friend?'

'Marie Ginoux.' I tell him who she is, that I've painted her, that I'm working on two or three new portraits of her.

'Sick?'

'Just like me,' I say. But she is not here, of course, so she is less sick than me, but it's the same melancholy. That's the word I use. I think he understands exactly what I mean.

We walk on in our embrace. 'What should I tell you about,' I say. 'My life story.'

'Yes.'

I feel very intimate with Franck. But even if so many things come to me to talk about, memories, feelings – I can still bring to mind the exact feelings from the past – of course it's still not a story with a life cycle and a character working its way to a final chord. It doesn't start in this or that place or at this or that moment, in order to end now in the south of France. I'm not Prado; that, in the past, I did or failed to do certain things doesn't mean anything for the present. My mother, I did tell Franck that, my mother told me about how, as a child, I looked at the others: 'Always from a distance, you didn't join in the conversation, you only got involved if there was really no other way. And you're still like that.' My sister was also like that, but my mother didn't mention that about her. My sister also always stood at a distance, but always next to my mother, that was her position, looking for protection, and protection she received.

I tell about how I could no longer live at home. Thrown out of the house. And I notice, *God damn it, that's how it goes*, that the following sentence almost bursts out of my mouth: 'And that's why I'm now here.' And if even I think that, then of course Franck also thinks it. But Franck moans for a moment and says: 'Me too.'

He left his parents at a lot younger age than me, he

says. 'But that's got nothing to do with anything.'

'There's no straight line in life,' I say.

'It can go any which way,' he says.

You can't explain anything, it's a matter of a gust of wind at one moment and a ray of sunshine at the next.

How long have we been going? The twilight has long since descended. Because of the fading light, the presence of our surroundings is becoming more and more noticeable. No geese here. Every time we see a rock looming up, we get nervous, but at each of those times we then find a flatter route, a little detour, which we take. And if we don't see it straight away we just stay there calmly puzzling over it until we've worked out a path.

The time that has passed in these mountains. They're only low mountains, but they look wild and majestic, especially from a distance. I've looked at them in the distance so many times from the window in my room.

We stop by a cypress tree. The tree is five metres tall, the wind in the branches, I remember the shuddering that I always felt. We allow for a few centimetres of space between us, Franck stands on one leg and tries to breathe calmly.

'Are you okay?' I say.

He nods.

From here on a slanting dirt road takes us to the institution along the fields.

Franck looks up.

Stars.

With our heads thrown back, we stand looking at them.

The wind rustling through the branches of the cypress tree, it seems as if it, too, can reach the stars.

It's pitch dark when we arrive. We walk along the wall, which we can't see, but which emits a salty odour and which we can follow just by imagining it. There's the fence. We stumble, but someone should come and help us any moment now. Or is everyone asleep? Maybe they did go out looking for us. Only when we're at the doorstep does someone come out of the kitchen, one of the helpers, and he, without asking anything, stand on Franck's other side and together we manoeuvre him up those two steps and go inside. Then Franck quickly gets taken over from me, without any fuss. Doctor Peyron takes him by the elbow and whispers some questions, another doctor comes along, he's lain down on a bed, I stay behind, exhausted. Exhausted, hungry. In the kitchen there are pans left with cold meat and cold soup and I scoop some up with a dirty spoon and take the plate and a piece of bread with me to the studio where I look at the paintings of Marie. Tomorrow I'll do some more work on them, and a self-portrait that's also there, because it makes our relationship clear. I can give them to her, together, when I'm in Arles.

With that thought, I go and look for Franck again. He's lying in bed like a corpse, but warm, with colour in his cheeks. He thanks me. Sleeping will help him to recover. The breathing. On the way to my room it springs to mind that I could have lain my hand on his head or on his shoulder, I could have whispered to him: 'It'll be okay.' It would have been true, it would have been appropriate, and it would have done Franck some good.

DECEMBER 1889

I imagine – I know that it's not true – the painters of Arles, the painters of the Studio, waiting for me. They have painted on and are expecting me back now; who knows what they've thought up: a banquet, a group portrait, or a day of working hard together, going out for the day, all together, with easels, canvases, 'Vincent, we have to take advantage of your presence.' How great that would be.

Then it would not be Franck who's taking me to the station, but Theo. And he would not only take me to the station, he would accompany me to Arles, the two brothers would arrive together and be welcomed by the painters of the South and the local population, gathered at the station. Merriment, this large group of faces and coats and hats and beards, waiting for us, they don't all fit onto the platform, they have to put their arms around each other's shoulders in order not to fall off it.

I haven't fantasised like this in a long time.

Franck isn't even limping any more. He says 'Bye,' walks back to the cart, lays his hand on the flank of the horse and climbs up on his seat. There they go. And I get onto the train and go and sit by the window of an almost empty carriage.

The train is set in motion, faster and faster. On our way.

The sky is inexhaustible. It's cloudless and the light is bright, but not sparkly, it is actually completely still, like water pushing on the bottom of a basin. On the bottom of a lake, an immeasurable bottom with small hills and large plateaus, and a web of paths with houses alongside and the track that runs directly across it. On that track is where I sit. I look out of the window. I see everything. Everything is dazzling. This landscape is the same as what I saw when I first arrived here, and I find it exactly as beautiful and hopeful and I imagine the same goings-on as then. I don't expect them any more, those goings-on, but it is still the landscape for artists and jokers and southerners. The setting for humorous and romantic stories.

I am being carried along by the bench, and that bench is being carried along by the train, all the way to Arles. I feel like waving.

And Arles I find just as beautiful and just as ugly as the first time. When I step off the train I suck in the fresh air which is still like pure water and I walk through the gate. I just saw the Rhône flowing, grey and blue, and now I'm walking through bumpy and restless streets towards the city, past Roulin's house, 'See you later,' I say in my mind, and then I'm nearly at the small square. I find it just as inviting as before.

Before.

I turn left when I'm on the square. The sky is now soft lilac and the air feels nice. I'm nearly at the small house. The little yellow house. I stand still but I can't look at it properly. That's because I'm tense, suddenly, now that I'm standing in the line of vision of possible passers-by; before you know it you can feel their eyes prodding your back. Later I'll come back. Go on, first to Marie.

Around the corner.

It's quiet, I'm almost the only one in the street.

The door of Café de la Gare. Closed.

I rattle on it. With my nose against the glass I try to peer into the darkness inside, but before I can make anything out someone is already opening the door. A pale man, ancient, who I've never seen before. Marie has died, crosses my mind. The man immediately leaves me alone again, this doesn't interest him. At the back I spot Joseph.

'Joseph,' I say.

He has a crate in his hands. He approaches me looking in towards the light.

'Vincent,' he says, 'what do you want?'

'I wrote to you, didn't I?'

'Yes, yes, yes.' He doesn't remember, but he lets me

in and points to a table and after a while puts a glass of cognac down in front of me. He's updating his stock. The old man and he are walking up and down with crates. I ask if I can help, but Joseph shakes his head and points to the table, as if to say: stay sitting there.

Marie is, of course, not dead, maybe she's feeling much better now, later Joseph will be able to tell me in peace. For me it's nice to sit for a while, I'm so tired now, my legs immediately relax. Apart from this, how is my body, is all well? It feels somehow arid on the inside, my skeleton needs greasing up, a dash of oil, but otherwise it's all right.

The stumbling and the pushing, the men panting in the half-darkness. The tables are all pushed to one side against the wall, the chairs are stacked one on top of the other. They want to tidy up, now it's very dusty, who is going to do that? Maybe Marie, if she's feeling better, maybe some women I don't know. I only know a few. After such a time. It was winter when I went away and now it's winter again. When you come back to a place after a long time, it's as if the space won't accept you, it's just like water that closes around you and propels you to the surface. First you have to talk for a bit, tell what's been happening and how it's going and then you achieve a bit of an agreement again. What is this dust, covering everything around here? Grains of sand from the square, of course, brought inside on shoes and boots, blown inside by the wind when the door was open. The fluff worn off from trousers and the other clothes of the visitors – of everyone in Arles, everyone who doesn't go to bed on time, at least – who shuffled their behinds on these chairs and padded their sleeves and rubbed their eyes. Cells. And waste, from peanuts and bread and shreds and sawdust. How long is it since they have cleaned the place? Not long, Jeanne helps with cleaning here as well, she used to do that before she came to our yellow house. But the lush dust buries everything in the blink of an eye.

My senses are raw as if I've just made it down from the top of a mountain.

It was a bad idea to come here. Or precisely the opposite. Stay calm. I've put my things against the table. Joseph will come and sit with me any moment now, then I'll see. I start taking the paintings out. It is too dark to be able to see the colours properly, maybe I should take them outside later for viewing, or maybe we won't look at them until we're upstairs. When Joseph finally comes to see me, he turns a chair backwards and slowly sits down, with legs wide apart and his elbows on the back of the chair. He's left the door to the annexe open, and a hazy light suddenly shines through it onto us.

'How are you?' he says.

'Up and down,' I say. 'More good than bad.'

'Good.'

'How is Marie?'

He moves his chin to the back. 'In bed. Not very well, more bad than good.' He sighs. 'I do everything around here on my own now.'

'I've brought something for Marie.' I stand up and get the canvases, which I can now show nicely in the light. I set each of the canvases against one leg, to do that I have to stand with my legs very wide apart and it makes me laugh, and Joseph too. There they are, I present them like my brother would to a buyer.

Joseph looks for a moment and says: 'If that's going to cheer her up...' and laughs again.

I laugh too.

He's red in the face from the exertion and he looks more muscular than before. His friendly, resolute figure is framed by the door opening – of course I fill it in – brown and red, fiery, that's how he blocks the way to Marie and the rest. His smile is forced and it makes him look unlikeable. But at other times his watery eyes look as if his thoughts have wandered away, free from the world around him, and that's when I like him the most. He doesn't say another word about the canvases, and that's good. We just talk. He gives me another cognac and I just let it happen. He's not looking at me most of the time, but when he does look, his eyes are calm. He isn't looking for signs of madness, like the others. Crazy Vincent or normal Vincent, it's all the same to him. He does notice that my clothes are cleaner. And that I'm wearing stiff shoes, in which I can only walk with difficulty. A painter. *And a painter brings along a painting, a painting of my wife, which everyone can see is strange, not beautiful, look at it. And you can't ask this fellow anything about it, especially not let him talk about it, because he'll think that you don't get it and then the following will happen: either he'll almost start to cry from despair, or he'll almost start to cry from rage.*

Are we going to stay here waiting until Marie is awake? I don't ask him, because Joseph won't make any decisions now, and then he might send me away.

Joseph shows me the new billiard table. It stands in the middle of the space in the back room, on massive, gleaming legs. In the frame around the cloth decorations have been carved out, white garlands in polished wood. 'Must've been expensive,' I say.

'What do you expect?' says Joseph.

We talk like that. Just when I want to start talking seriously about Marie, he abruptly turns around. 'Just leave those paintings there. Marie can look at them when she's awake. Isn't that a good idea? A good idea. This afternoon. Then you can come back this afternoon.'

I leave feeling somewhat relieved. Coming back this afternoon, that might mean a new beginning. Everything may look different. The small square is still empty. The even light makes everything motionless. It is just as if all life exists in nooks and crannies and I fantasise about having to go searching for people and then finding them in caves, where they sit together by the light of the fire and make music. But I'm standing in front of Joseph's café, the sensation has disappeared again.

Marie is lying somewhere up there. Maybe she's heard me, maybe she's happy and a bit comforted and wants to

109

pep herself up quite a bit before this afternoon. 'We are both ill,' I will say, 'but look, just like me, you'll also get better.'

Still, it would have been better to have seen Marie now, so that I could have paid her a nice visit, and the convivial atmosphere of that would have set the tone for the rest of the day: maybe they would have offered me a meal, other people would have come round for a chat, Roulin perhaps, and then life in the café would continue in its normal lively way, with me part of it.

I go to Roulin's.

He might not be there, but if he is he'll put his arm round my shoulder. To see the children, who he will tickle to make them laugh in front of me. The tiny room which is way too full and which we will quickly leave because Roulin and I can't stand the tightness any more, will do me good, like a nap. Maybe it's like that.

No, I should first look for Rachel, after all. It's still early now. This is what I was thinking: if I go early, there is a chance. The early hour cools down all excitement and fear, in her and the patron and the other girls, and I will act sober too – some short remarks, apologies, asking how she is. Not talk about anything, delivering no stories. In that case I have to go now. Only I don't go past the café and across the square, then they'll think I'm walking around in circles. I go through the city, past the arena.

And after I've been to Rachel, I'll go and eat something, and then back to Marie. That's the day's programme.

It's not cold any more. The wind has stopped. It makes no sense to run, *I'm just having a walk around, people.* Just shot through the landscape on a train, and now here in all calmness. I walk past the arena where, when there are festivities, masses of people swarm in, into the ring, and are later pushed back out, but where now, fortunately, emptiness reigns. The square around the arena is just at the top of a slight hill. Here and there a woman, and a child. Two older men. I don't know them, and they don't know me.

110

But now that we are sharing the street with one another as individuals, we naturally greet each other, I have to clear my throat for it.

Because of the fresh smell of the stone and the unspoilt air, the idea of a hostile community, of the residents of Arles snapping their pincers at me like lobsters, fades away from my mind. But something else starts building up. The impenetrability of their lives, the realisation that their inner self and mine can only bump against each other, and that we will never be able to come closer than that. In the narrow street in front of me a girl is walking, it's so narrow that she's basically blocking my way, and it is Jeanne. She's wearing a dress with ribbons of rough material, in blue and red, that looks cheerful on her, the work and the cold didn't stop her from looking like that.

To the side. My first inclination is to silently let her pass. She probably won't say anything either, she starts and then anxiously ignores me. That's how it goes, if she's scared then it's actually a good deed to pretend I don't know her. She's carrying a bucket of water. She has to change hands and hold the bucket diagonally in front of her, the splashing weight pulls her shoulders downwards and as compensation she tries to lift her head.

Have I always paid her for her cleaning work? No idea, Gauguin did that.

'Bonjour, Mr Vincent,' she says.

'Bonjour,' I say. Because I wanted to walk on, I have to keep my distance now. Have to – it goes without saying, even if I don't actually want to any more. I draw myself up to my full height and feign being occupied, in a hurry.

'Mr Vincent, are you back or is it just temporary?'

'Temporary.'

'Is Mr Gauguin also here?'

'No,' I say, 'Mr Gauguin isn't with me. He is in Paris. Why?'

That's what always happens! If I've decided to do something, I can't walk away any longer, I'm chained to one particular track, and that leads to this discomfort – discomfort, that's what Theo calls it, and mother too: everyone feels uncomfortable with you – look, that's ferocity in Jeanne's eyes.

Now I'm standing here thinking about it and didn't hear what she said.

'Pardon. He had promised me something,' she says.

Mr Vincent is so haughty, and on what grounds? Living like an animal, without earning money, no wife, ill and crazy. And then to act so superciliously. He does look a bit better, calmer than before, but he'll have to pay, there's no one to take the blame for him, he won't get away with it this time. Walking around, not doing anything. Making a mess. And then letting other people clean up after him.

She thinks that Gauguin and I are still connected. But no, we could actually hardly be further removed from each other. If this had gone differently, then Marie would have received me this morning. That's how it is. And then Jeanne wouldn't have been scared, or maybe still scared but in a good way. With Gauguin at my side. Or with Theo, or Milliet, or Franck…

I can tell Jeanne that I'll write to Gauguin and can pass on her message. But then I have to be quick, she's almost around the corner. I walk after her, she feels that, naturally, but doesn't turn around. To tap her on the shoulder, impossible. I'll just say her name, really softly.

'Jeanne.'

I'm going to offer to carry that bucket for her. Offer my apologies. And offer my help with Gauguin. But she speeds up. She has to hold her bucket steady with two hands. If she could run, she would. It goes wrong so quickly, so quickly everything is beyond mending. As if I'm going to do something to her. There is a magnet that pulls all my intentions and words to one side, it is invisible and it is there in every conversation and in every contact.

I have the urge to kick the bucket out of her hands. I'll give you a reason to be scared.

Straight on.

To the left.

The maze of alleyways, the solid crooked shadows, the city indeed looks as if it's cut up into pieces. I remember the mistral that used to blow so often. The streets would shelter you from it, but sometimes they formed wind passages and you'd nearly get blown away. The gusts around your head. The chilliness that could wash over you on the warmest of days.

If I carry on walking now, I'll arrive at Rachel's in a minute. But I want to calm down. I enter the first café I come across, order a cognac and sit down on a small chair by the brown wall. Because it will go wrong. And oh, they'll see it all happen. You see, Jeanne will say, I predicted it all. I feel a fuse burning, crackling. I'll be dragged along as if I'm asleep, dragged along in a nightmare again. Maybe I should run away. Yes, I have to get up and run away immediately, without saying goodbye to Marie, that's just how it is then, it went wrong but I can limit the damage. Franck, come and get me.

The door is open. I can walk inside, but I've set my mind on ringing the doorbell and this situation will be easier: I stand on one side, the patron on the other, we talk calmly and the patron decides in the end if he will permit a meeting with Rachel. And so, if he allows it, I'll stand opposite her. What do I do now? I knock on the open door and with one foot on the doorstep, wait for a reaction. The small porch is screened off with a blue curtain. Suddenly that curtain is pulled open and the patron sticks his head into the small hallway. He sees me, but nothing else, I'm not what he's looking for. He throws the curtain shut again. Now I can't walk on. There's something going on inside, I have to wait until the situation is solved, in this little box that smells of rain but at least is warm. But what is happening? Maybe I'll have to wait for hours. Then I hear a woman screaming, two women, probably. It sounds angry, with a panicky undertone. One woman shouts in a rough voice, she wants to get her way. I then hear, 'Give! Give! Give!' but that sounds as if it's moved further down in the building. Now the man is also shouting, in an almost friendly way, as if he's standing at the bottom of the stairs, calling the guests on the upper floor. Then suddenly a warm animal crashes into me. Rachel.

She's stormed in through the curtain and is staring at me, bewildered. I flatten myself against the wall to let her pass, it feels like I haven't taken a breath for about an hour, if only because of that I cannot say anything to her now, go on, I gesture. Dressed in a red robe and with long loose hair, she looks at me with fiery eyes – fiery, seething. Then she charges at me. Her fists crashing against my chest.

Strike.

She keeps on hitting me, for no reason. It's so good to feel that, the jealousy, to be standing so close to her, fighting with her, her arms and legs striking me and her blustering breath on my face. I feel no pain. Just how she hits me and grabs me and claws at me. The last time I felt her, in bed, it wasn't as close as this, even if we were naked and touching each other, like someone stroking your hair. My God.

She steps back. She looks. She's almost as tall as me.

Then she strikes.

I duck down and block with my lower arm and when I turn back I notice that the blow actually was stopped, but my arm is burning and with her other fist Rachel now punches me in the stomach. Not hard. Too tired.

Rachel laughs and gasps.

We look at each other like that. I laugh too.

'Go on,' I say.

And with her red coat she goes off, as if on a broomstick.

Where am I? I gasp and laugh for a bit longer, alone in the little hallway, as if I've woken up from a dream. I need a moment to orientate myself. Then I also step outside.

In the narrow street in front of the brothel there are

two options, left and right. Just as I decide to go left, I see Rachel standing by a corner on the right. She moves a few steps towards me, and then, from a distance, quickly waves. And she's gone again.

Who knows where to. I'm free. I'm still a bit stunned, but like that, the way she was standing there, that's how I need to paint her. Don't forget! Don't forget!

God damn it, here I am walking again. Up this street, down another, go outside, the Crau, into the field, at least that's over in St Remy, but in Arles I've always walked from pillar to post, always dragging myself through the dust the whole bloody day.

I wait for the explosion. The warning signs are there, the whirlpools in my head, the sweating in the cold. Those whirlpools – those things I normally can't talk about because they disappear when I talk to people like Jeanne and Marie and Benoît and everyone. Until now it's always happened with an explosion. I sometimes don't recognise it until afterwards, but still I remember it every time: a crash, a fountain of stars and then hell.

Ah... ah, there is Theo walking along. Turns into a street, where is he going? Quickly, I'll lose him soon. How can that be, he has so much to do. Did he come to visit me? The thin brown jacket that flutters around him loosely never suited him, he still hasn't bought a new one. How incredibly lovely if that's really you, Theo, even if of course it's nonsense that he has come, why wouldn't he have written then? This is one of those sensations, hallucinations. Not true but it seems to be real. Or true enough, but incomprehensible.

Theo, on his way to the square, my own square by my own house. That would be something. I also have to go there. This urge, that I've been feeling this whole time. To the square. Is that where it's going to happen?

It's busier now in the Café de la Gare. The door is held open by a stool, people are walking in and out. Hustle and bustle. That makes it easier, I just have to step inside and there's a chance I'll blend in with the company immediately. There's a lot of noise, voices, singing, someone's shouting. As I move further into the café, nothing changes. The population, thirty or forty men, continue their conversations, eyes directed at each other, ready to laugh at a joke, or with eyes already narrowed from enjoyment. There are still some plates and glasses on the tables, but everyone has stood up after lunch, found reasons to stay, mainly so as not to go away. I tower over everybody. I see Joseph, who is the only one standing still in that lively mess. He's wiping his hands. He glances to the right and back, straight in front of him, whilst he's long since noticed me. To his right, the paintings are standing on the floor, they stand out against the grey panelling in the matt gaslight.

I walk over to them.

No.

Someone's written words in a scrawl with black paint over the canvases. With red paint they've made stains around my head, I immediately understand, they must represent drops of blood. And they've painted over Marie's portrait in white paint, effaced it in broad brushstrokes. On the white surface they have drawn tiny animals, a pig, a cow, with big pricks.

'Joseph,' I say.

No, I don't say that, I just think it. I turn. Now Joseph laughs and walks up to me.

'Come on,' he says, 'come on.' Now he's laughing aloud, roaring with laughter, his look is uncomfortable but not for long, more men are laughing now and pushing forwards and looking at me greedily. I can picture them at it. I can picture it, a palette of faces, red and white and honey-coloured, those grimaces, and everyone sticks out their hand and puts on a dab of paint, a dab of paint onto the canvas. They feel the resistance of the jute against the brush. And Marie too, that pale face towering over the others is hers, her arm stretched and she doesn't just put on a dab of paint, no, she swings her arm backwards from the shoulder, her whole arm and torso move together, like a bullfighter she lashes the paint, her bullfighter expression mocking everything.

'Come on,' Joseph says.

Out, out, I'm being thrown out.

It didn't happen like that, it didn't have to happen like that. Sober up.

Sober up.

But it's true, isn't it? This is what I see. Jesus sees love, God sees your worth in the world, Franck sees the work that needs to be done, my father sees everything that's wrong and I see this.

Where am I going? Now I am indeed criss-crossing the city, but I shouldn't swerve through the streets like this. To the Rhône, the wide water. Or to the PLM site, that's a good idea, go there. To hide, yes, I realise it only now, but that's exactly what I'll do there: hide in one of the shepherds' huts where the Italians also hid. If it happens there, it won't be so bad. Maybe I can sleep there, or stay a few days. Because it's going to happen, it won't be long, when I crash land again in a nightmare.

All my thoughts, all my ideas, the smallest memories that are swirling around inside me like schools of fish, all that I want to do, want to paint, it is a fire which burns in me, but they see only a puff of smoke, moreover a gust of smoke that blows away. And then? Then the fire, of course, is also gone.

I'm being pushed to the square. They're all doing it, everyone, Rachel and Jeanne and Joseph and even Gauguin, he is, I think, also on the square, even if that's impossible, but I'm also doing it myself, like someone with a fear of heights who has to jump into the deep. Don't go. Make sure you don't go anywhere, sit on the ground.

117

If it goes wrong later, they absolutely shouldn't think that it's because of the paintings, because of the rape of my paintings. They will think that. Benoît thinks: haha, drove him to the edge just like that, and Michel, God damn it, that one would love nothing more than to come and stand in front of me and slap me on the cheeks, like a child, *look at him losing it, look at him losing it.*

Look, they will say, first harassing Rachel, and then the drinking, and the fight with Gauguin, and abandoning his brother. You could see it coming. It was going to happen, you could predict it, everything was leading up to this moment.

How can I make it clear that it's a lie?

Lie? Look, then, at how it is with him, look. Now he has to pay.

I have to pay.

And now I'm here, you see. It's going to happen here, indeed, maybe it's good that I made my way to the little square, we can't postpone it any longer.

Once we're in the square, it seems much, much bigger. In fact it's not small at all, now that it's this full of people. Yes, it's flooded with people. Dozens, hundreds of people, almost everyone from Arles must be here. Boys have climbed into the bare trees to get a better view. They keep a space free in the middle. They come to look at me, or listen. To see the crash. It's not here yet, but you can feel it. Waiting for the thunder.

Fool.

Look at this. Two men are standing in the empty space in the square, next to a collection of pieces of wood. First they erect the two posts, kept together at the top by a log containing the knife. That's the knife of a guillotine. I would have thought that this knife, the weapon itself, would be separately raised, wrapped up in a cloth, or maybe a flag, and, loaded with terror and veneration, secured at the peak. But no, the knife is the core and the beginning of everything. The wood is painted red. Of course. On both sides the men are fixing planks. They're doing it in complete silence, they've performed this task countless times. Then the small bench on which I later have to lie. Another upright plank, the function of which I don't understand, is being secured in front of the bench. The men are moving an oxen-yoke in two separate parts between the poles. Ropes, hinges, a large basket into which the body will flop down via a folded-out slide. The lid of the basket will flap open towards the audience, the little ones won't even be able to look over it. On the other side now stand two big bags of water. Death is a practical matter.

No joking, my man. No joking.

The people are standing around, chattering. Gauguin is there too. He's standing on the right, with his buttoned-up jacket, not talking to anyone. He looks a bit frightened, by his standards. Of course he wants to see it, I do understand that. He must have just come back from Paris, where they are for ever talking about the 'enigmatic paintings' that he made here in Arles – that's what they call them there and, God damn it, they are right. That's what he thinks, that they were right, I don't think that, for me those paintings are his best to date.

Why is he here? His plan to live off Theo and me has failed, he's like a woman who has latched onto a rich man and yet didn't manage to get any inheritance. Always chasing after money. He looks tired, with that big head he has to keep holding up. He's looking at me intently. Now, approximately now, he would have wanted to leave for the tropics, to lead the life of a savage. He can't wait any longer, otherwise he'd grow too weak here in France to change anything at all. Of course he wants to see death. Maybe out of a feeling of guilt, maybe he thinks his guilt can be absolved through facing death, through meeting someone who's dying. He wants to see death and thinks that it will be something subtle, one of the tiniest moments, you have to do your best for it, and he's doing his best. Maybe I should give him a sign but I don't know which sign.

Just let his plans fail.

Theo is standing there – indeed, he is here, the man in that coat really was him. He looks sad, tired too, but also strong, and I'm not connected to anyone as I am to him.

He would help me if he could. But that's not possible.

To the left, on the other side, stand the Italians I haven't seen for such a long time, but in their eyes I see that they remember exactly who I am: the man who chased them out of the city with his friends. If they could they would slap me in the face with an open palm, and I wish they would, that they'd hit me for my cowardly cruelty and then afterwards embrace me. Benoît and Michel are standing next to them. Marie has come out, wrapped in a blanket. She's standing next to Gauguin, and I see them catching up a bit, but not about me, because they wouldn't understand each other, and Marie soon walks on for a little way. She is ill, but she is going to win. Gauguin is a guide, but not for me, not as long as he's standing there on the side.

My parents, my sister, no, father obviously not. Mother blinks her eyes at me for a second, as if to wish me all the best. They disappear into the crowd.

Suddenly seven men appear. Men in top hats, long coats. One of them, the executioner, he can't be anything else, is wearing a white collar and a lighter grey jacket. The others come, one by one, to stand next to him, sometimes in little groups, laughing. They're waiting. How aggravating, this waiting, why wait? Put an end to the affair, everything is ready. The executioner is standing with his arms behind his back in the open space, with his hat, his moustache and a smile on his ruddy face, like a host. His legs, forming a slight x, firmly anchor him. His trouser legs fall over his shoes. He's feeling as fit as a fiddle. He has a full beard. And his pals swarming around him.

I slowly walk forwards. Because I have been standing still, my legs have stiffened even more. There are men walking along behind me, staff maybe, gendarmes.

God, now it's real – these people here have all seen

me at some point, but now it's really all about me – as if some devastating promise is being fulfilled. Do all of these people have this sensation? Maybe not, plenty of them are too drunk to be able to tell what exactly is going on, but Theo, and Joseph and Marie over there. And for Gauguin the sensation is so strong, he's bending forward as if he's received a blow to the liver. Where is Milliet?

Milliet.

'Hurry up,' says one of the men.

I say: 'My legs are tied, arsehole.'

Prado.

The sun, the sky. The trees on the square, as sharp as glass. The people who stand waiting. Gauguin whispers 'God damn it', it's so quiet that I hear it. Marie's gasping breath. My mother hooks her arm around my sister's, fabric against fabric. Michel is snorting because he can barely hold in laughter. Jeanne. Rachel disappeared. Soon everything will sink away.

Actually, I have to find the words now and tell all these folk, all these good and bad citizens who understand each other so well, who I am, about my youth, my parents, memories of loneliness and longing, everything, just tell them. But these memories are now simply unretrievable, inside me there's only a thick pulp, and if you look at it for too long, if you hunt for something within it to bring out into daylight, everything dissolves.

I'm frozen.

My lips are open, the cooling air fills up my mouth and throat cavities.

Four men grip me tightly and push me against the upright plank. The wood comes up to the top of my chest and I'm scared that it will press into my throat, my Adam's apple. Now I know what that plank is for: my weight will topple it over onto a hinge – I'm falling, I'm falling – I'm lying flat on my stomach, my God, and they shove me into position. The plank carries me and they carry the plank forwards. Hands grip my legs tight, someone holds both of my ears (he has to grab twice) and the wood is clasped around my neck.

Seconds go by. Seconds that consist of hundreds, thousands of seconds. I'm lying a bit head-first, with my legs slightly up. The weight of my body shifts forwards, maybe a centimetre, and presses against the wood of my neck clasp. This balance completely occupies me. The light feeling in my head, as if I am in a free fall. My mouth is open. When I take a breath, the cold air sticks a balloon through my mouth into my chest. Suddenly a thought grabs hold of me: my blood is swelling up, as if I was caught red-handed doing something awful, but that's not it, I'm going to die and my blood is not swelling up but losing its strength and sinking away into my dry flesh.

That thought disappears. My body completely relaxes.

It is half-dark, so quiet. I feel a soft wind against my cheeks and my ears.

There is nothing.

There are images. A hound. A hand. The smell of Himalayan balsam, voices in the air. All the hope that I've ever felt in me, all the true hope. That's there. There is so much. I want to scream out loud. All these people are still standing around me, it's my last chance, but the knife now thunders down. I hear it moving through the air as if it's splitting ice, but I don't want to hear the crash, I want to shout, my head is fixed but I wriggle my body so that I can at least look, I want to shout, a centimetre free, two centimetres, I can turn, and then the knife cuts through – not my neck, but my jaw and my skull.

It feels as if a veil is being pulled out of me, a veil of the thinnest, most poisonous fire.

My skull plonks to the ground. Someone grabs it by the hair, to show to the crowd, of course. The wine-red blood, bits of rubbish from the street are already getting stuck to it. But he quickly drops me again, because my mutilated skull is too gruesome to display.

Two boys roll me into a large basket. The basket is being closed. I feel them lifting up the basket. Keeping it up in the air. Leaning it to the side. Laying it down. Onto the cart, the cart I saw earlier. And after some hours the cart starts moving. Hours?

The carriage travels for hours. You can hear the horses. First really slow, then they find a rhythm.

I'm being carried in a basket and that basket is in a cart and the cart is being pulled by horses.

At the front of the cart sits a man driving the horses. Occasionally he turns towards me.

After a few hours he notices something about me and starts to talk.

'It's me,' he says.

I look at him.

'It's me, Franck. Just stay calm. Go to sleep. I've come to get you.'

I say nothing.

The Author

Jeroen Blokhuis is a Dutch author and a communications advisor.

He has published short stories in literary magazines including *Passionate* en *KortVerhaal*. He has also written booklets for educational publishers and professional publications about content strategy.

His short story 'Vroeger' ('The Past') was published in Dutch and English in the Holland Park Press online magazine in 2012. The basis for this short story was a short screenplay written ten years ago which won the Gouden Vlam screenplay prize.

His debut novel *Place Lamartine* was published in Dutch in September 2015 and *The Yellow House* translated by Asja Novak is the English version of this novel.

More details are available from

www.hollandparkpress.co.uk/blokhuis

THE TRANSLATOR

Asja Novak was born in 1993 in Croatia.

In 2008 she moved to London to study art and languages She has a degree in History of Art and Dutch and studied Dutch language at the largest Centre for Dutch Studies in the English -speaking world based at UCL.

She is currently immersed in literary theory and translation. Her background in arts and languages makes her an ideal translator of *The Yellow House* by Jeroen Blokhuis, which is her first professional translation project.

She lives and works in Utrecht, the Netherlands.

Holland Park Press is a unique publishing initiative. Its aim is to promote poetry and literary fiction, and discover new writers. It specializes in contemporary English fiction and poetry, and translations of Dutch classics. It also gives contemporary Dutch writers the opportunity to be published in Dutch and English.

To

- Learn more about Jeroen Blokhuis
- Discover other interesting books
- Read our unique Anglo-Dutch magazine
- Find out how to submit your manuscript
- Take part in one of our competitions

Visit www.hollandparkpress.co.uk

Bookshop: http://www.hollandparkpress.co.uk/books.php

Holland Park Press in the social media:

http://www.twitter.com/HollandParkPres
http://www.facebook.com/HollandParkPress
https://www.linkedin.com/company/holland-park-press
http://www.youtube.com/user/HollandParkPress